THE
MYSTERY
OF
HOLLOW
PLACES

THE MYSTERY OF HOLLOW PLACES

REBECCA PODOS

Balzer + Bray
An Imprint of HarperCollinsPublishers

Balzer + Bray is an imprint of HarperCollins Publishers.

The Mystery of Hollow Places

www.epicreads.com

Library of Congress Cataloging-in-Publication Data
Podos, Rebecca.
       The mystery of hollow places / Rebecca Podos. — First edition.

              pages   cm
       Summary: A mystery writer's daughter sets out to find her missing father and, along the way, begins to understand the loneliness that has gripped them both since her mother abandoned them years before.
       ISBN 978-0-06-237334-2 (hardback)
       [1. Mystery and detective stories.   2. Missing persons—Fiction.   3. Mothers—Fiction.]   I. Title.
PZ7.1.P63My   2016   2015010331
[Fic]—dc23   CIP
                                                                  AC

15 16 17 18 19   PC/RRDH   10 9 8 7 6 5 4 3 2 1

❖

First Edition

For Mom and Dad—

Thanks for the books. I love you and whatever.

THE
MYSTERY
OF
HOLLOW
PLACES

ONE

The bedtime story my dad used to tell me began with my grandmother's body.

Back when my dad wasn't yet my dad, but a young forensic pathologist at Good Shepherd Hospital in the city, a dead woman landed on his table. She was middle-aged and unremarkable, her hair colorless, her face like a vacant moon. Gone already when the ambulance brought her in, she'd died in a park in the evening, quietly and alone. After she was cleaned and scraped and stripped, my dad performed the autopsy. A run-of-the-mill operation until he dug down deep and found her heart.

It wasn't the bloody blue thing he'd expected, but a pocked stone the size of his fist. As he lifted it to snip it loose, the veins crumbled away from it, turned to dust. My dad held the heart to the light, rapped on it gently with his knuckles, then locked it in his desk drawer until early the next morning, when he came back with a rock hammer and chisel bought from a hardware store a few blocks away. He laid a blue cloth across the exam table—the kind they use to cover bodies—and settled the heart on the cloth. Hands sweaty inside his surgical gloves, he turned it over until he found a dark seam in the stone. Carefully, he slotted the chisel against it, and with a *chink*, *chink*, *chink*, *CRACK*, the heart split in two. Inside the thick gray rind of rock there were no vessels, or tissues, or anything warm. Instead, a pocket of crystals like clear teeth winked up at him. This happened, he knew from his school days; with enough time and the right conditions, precious stones could grow in hollow places.

Weeks later, the dead woman's daughter was finally tracked down. She'd been studying abroad in Switzerland. She was brought to my dad in the Good Shepherd morgue to claim the body in the cooler. He showed her pictures of the dead woman, taken when the ambulance ferried her in. The daughter shook her head. She hadn't seen her mother in years beyond counting; this could be anyone's mother.

My dad showed her the shabby dress the dead woman had worn, the chipped jewelry, the low-heeled shoes. Still the daughter shook her head. None of it was familiar.

At last, he unlocked the desk drawer and took out the stone heart, wrapped many times over in the big blue cloth, which smelled always of formaldehyde and earth. When he placed the halves in the daughter's hands, her face crumpled. "Yes, this is her," the daughter said softly. "She was a lonely woman."

He plucked a tissue from the box, then turned back and saw tears glittering on her round cheeks and her unpainted lips, and the way she clutched the heart with one small hand and her long brown hair with the other. In that moment, he said, he knew for certain he was looking at my mother.

When my stepmother became my stepmother, I asked her if she knew about the heart. By then, Dad hadn't mentioned it or shown it to me for years. I'm not sure why I brought it up, except to prove to Lindy that we had plenty of stories before she came along, stories she played no part in. But my stepmother sat my father and me down that evening and persuaded him to tell me the whole truth.

After my grandmother died in the park by Good Shepherd Hospital, Dad said, he devoted himself to my mother. He married her in the spring and moved them out of the city, into a quiet house with many windows and few doors. He left the morgue early each night and brought her presents—a candy bar from the vending machine, daisies from a flower stand at the train and bus station in Sugarbrook. Dad loved my mother so much he felt his heart would split, and then I was born and I was loved by both of them. But my mother grew sad, stiff, and cold, like her mother before her. ("Nothing to do with you, Immy," Lindy interrupted. "It was just in her chemistry.") One night, my mother left us, taking a suitcase, no money, and half of the heart with her. She sent the divorce papers through a process server a little while later. Of course Dad was sorry, but he had his daughter to think of. Ready to put the past behind him, he quit his job at Good Shepherd, trading his scalpel and surgical gloves for pens and paperweights.

This much I knew already. My father writes popular medical mysteries, the kind you read in airports. Since I was little I've been sneaking his books into my room, books with thick spines and blood spatters on the covers, and reading them under my blanket. They're all about a handsome forensic pathologist who solves deaths that seem extraordinary but are in fact perfectly explainable. Someone poisoned the dead man's salmon fillet, or switched the dead woman's asthma medicine with dry ice. Nobody's organs ever turn to stone. There's no magic in his books at all.

But I believed my dad about the heart. I still believe. He had proof—the half left behind—and though I haven't seen it in forever, I remember it perfectly. A semicircle of gray stone, its inside sharp with small crystals. He would show it to me at night and, sitting in my nest of stuffed bears, I'd run one finger over the roughness of it. "It wasn't your mother's fault," Dad would say with a sigh, "or her mother's. The women in that family were cursed. They could be lonely wherever they were. But not us, Immy. We have each other. So we'll never, ever have to feel that way."

As he spoke, Dad cradled our piece of the rock, which I was never allowed to hold. He clasped it to his own chest as if to protect it, as if it weren't already broken.

TWO

It's after ten on Thursday night when Lindy hands Officer Griffin her second cup of coffee. While they talk, I
splash what's left in the pot into my own *Mystery Writers of America* mug. It's thick and semicool and tastes
like horribly burned toast. Dad has always been the master of coffee in this house. That's how it works: Lindy
is the appointment keeper, the bills mailer, the tax filer,
while Dad's the coffee maker, the grocery shopper, the
homework checker. At the moment my homework sits
upstairs untouched, my English essay blank but for my
name, date, and class number. I'm not worried. Lindy
will write me a note. Something like:

Dear Mr. McCormick,

Please excuse Imogene Scott's incomplete home-work. We were up late filing a missing persons report for Immy's father, and the time just got away from us.

Sincerely,

Lindy Scott

Fanned out across the kitchen table are pictures of Dad taken in the past few years. Officer Griffin examines the black-and-white headshot from the back cover of his latest novel, *No Shirt, No Pulse, No Problem.* Dad is sitting in his home office behind a fortress of books and weird paperweights and framed photos, miniature Lindys and Imogenes unidentifiable in their smallness. He chews the stem of a pipe and stares into the distance, as if a story is writing itself while he waits for the click of the camera. If this picture were to wash up on a foreign shore years from now and a stranger plucked it out of the sand, they'd think Dad was some pompous literary great. But he isn't either of those things. It isn't even a real pipe in the headshot, just a plastic joke pipe I bought him in honor of his tenth published book. It blows goddamn bubbles.

How could anyone recognize him from this picture?

Officer Griffin sets the headshot down gently and turns to her notebook, where for two hours she's been taking notes such as: a description of the individual (tall-ish, pale-ish, gray-ish hair, half Asian-ish, fifty-ish, Dad-ish), full name (Joshua Zhi Scott), last known location (his bed, beside Lindy, Wednesday night), known locations frequented by the individual (the local Starbucks, his home office, whichever of our two and a half bathrooms has whatever book he's currently reading in the rack beside the toilet), means of travel available to the individual (he left his car and credit card behind, but according to the bank, withdrew $1,500 two days ago—so pretty much any means).

As I slip into my seat she turns to me.

"You're a senior in high school, Imogene?"

"At Sugarbrook High, yeah."

"Tough year. College applications, SATs, prom dates . . ."

"Immy's in the honor society," Lindy jumps in. "And mock trial, aren't you?"

"That's great! What colleges have you applied to?"

"Um, Emerson? And Amherst and BU. And Simmons."

"Local schools, huh?"

"I want to be close to home. My friend's brother even commutes from home, and he likes it." Beneath the table I wrap my right fist around my left thumb, just above the knuckle, and pull until it cracks. I do the same with each finger one by one, a nervous habit Dad says will one day require that my ruined joints be replaced by a robot hand.

The officer nods. "Sure. I told my own daughter how nice it'd be for her to stay local, but she can't wait to get across the country. Bet your parents are real proud of you."

I shrug.

"Is he in the habit of pulling you from school, your dad?"

"No," Lindy says at once. "Absolutely not."

"Uh-huh." Officer Griffin jots a note. "So why'd he take you out yesterday, do you think?"

"Um. I don't know. It was a nice day?"

My first half truth. Wednesday was sunny but cold, capped by a brilliant blue sky that never lived up to its promise. That morning I crawled from bed, prepared as always to spend half an hour bullying my straight, dark hair into almost-waves; to make a desperate swipe at eye makeup only to rub it all off self-consciously; to shun whatever outfit had seemed cool the night before and rummage hopelessly through my closet; to sprint out the door with a granola bar between my teeth and home- work and car keys trailing behind me; to sputter into

Sugarbrook High's senior parking lot in my unreliable little Civic with three minutes to spare. Except before all of that, Dad headed me off at the pass. When I slumped out into the hall on my way to the bathroom, he was waiting.

"How are you feeling today, Immy?" he asked.

I blinked. While Lindy was usually out the door for work by the time I'd punched the snooze button, it was rare to find Dad awake before I left for school. Stranger still, he was dressed, with his glasses on, furrows from the comb's teeth still fresh in his smoothed-back hair. His eyes, very dark and shaped like Ma Ma Scott's, like mine, were bright and alert.

"Hummuh?" I groaned.

"I'm just checking, because you don't look well."

"Grur," I wheezed.

"What I'm saying is, if you weren't feeling up to school, I'd sympathize. I don't want you going in sick."

"Are you . . . saying I don't have to go to school?"

Dad shrugged and stared out the window, where the sky was flushing pink in the east. "It's supposed to be a great day. The first nice day in months. I was just thinking it'd be a shame to waste it. Unless you've got a test or something?"

I shook my head. Dad had never made an offer like this. He was a big one for education. I knew he'd worked through four years of premed, four years of med school, four years of clinical training and residency, and all this before I was born. I don't even remember his long days in the lab at Good Shepherd, before he gave it up. Staying home sick was hard enough—even if he was out of practice, he could still sniff out a fake flu in the time it took me to blow my nose. And staying home just because? Unheard of.

I asked, "Are *you* sure you're okay?"

"Always. I just, you know, I thought we could spend some time together. Catch up."

So he called the school while I dressed, a little dazed. It wasn't normal, but I wasn't about to turn down a day off. Maybe because it was the last school week before February break, and he'd caught the same bug us students had.

As it happened, Dad had a plan. We got on I-95 North and after forty-something miles of Bob Dylan and CCR on Boston's oldies station we took the off-ramp toward Newbury. By that time I'd figured out where we were headed: Victory Island.

There are dozens and dozens of beachy day-trip towns in Massachusetts, and countless more along the East Coast, but Victory Island is ours. Brick-laid walking paths wind between candle shops, toy shops, cheese shops. *Fish and Chips* is scrawled on the chalkboard menus of every bar and restaurant. Then there's the water. Cleaner than Revere and far less crowded than the Nantucket beaches, Victory Island Beach is sandy and sloping. The water is cold even in the haziest, hottest summer, and almost impossible to ease into. Ten feet from the shore and you're up to your shoulders.

Dad parked in the sandy lot down the street. There wasn't a parking attendant, and there wouldn't be for months yet. Obviously we hadn't bothered with swimsuits or towels—according to the little electric thermometer on the rearview mirror, it was hovering below fifty—so I didn't have much baggage. Just my sunglasses and coat and a book I'd snatched from my nightstand, rushing so Dad wouldn't change his mind. Dad rummaged in the trunk and came up with the ragged quilt he kept for roadside emergencies.

We crossed one of the boardwalks between dunes furred with beach grass and turned left down the rockier stretch of sand. Dad laid out the quilt and I huddled down on it in my jacket. It was a glassy, just-thawed kind of cold. Brisk wind stirred grit over the blanket, into our laps, and between my teeth when I talked. At least it was too early for the mosquitoes and greenhead flies that plagued the beach in summer. The water spread out in front of us, a flat bruise-blue. I snuck down to the wet sand and stuck a finger in the shallows and shrieked despite myself. The cold of it was like fire.

Back at the blanket, I crossed my arms over my growling stomach. It's a long drive from Sugarbrook, and it was lunchtime already. "Did we bring any food or anything?" I asked, though one look around and you could see Dad hadn't. Not even a Ziploc bag of Lucky Charms in his pocket, his usual breakfast.

"Oops, no. I guess it slipped my mind. We'll grab something in town later, huh?"

While Dad sat with his arms around his knees, I hunkered down against the blanket and tried to read my book. Tried to reread it, actually. *Rebecca,* by Daphne du Maurier, is one of my all-time beloved darling favorites. You know how there are precious books you hold like eggs or something, and you only read them in special places when you want to feel like a grown-up, and you wash your hands so you won't blotch them with your terrible human fingers? *Rebecca* isn't one of those. It's stained with Pepsi and pen ink and makeup from rattling around the bottom of every backpack I've owned. The spine is cracked from me falling asleep on it. The fifth chapter has fallen out all apiece, so I use an alligator clip to keep it in the book when I'm not reading. My love is killing it. It's so good that even people who look down their noses at genre stuff still call it a "modern classic." But really it's just an awesome mystery. It's about a girl who goes to work in Monte Carlo and is wooed by Maximilian de Winter, a handsome, super-rich Englishman who marries her after two weeks (the thirties were a different time). They move to his giant mansion in Manderley, where the girl meets the house-keeper, who turns out to be horrible, a shrew who's obsessed with Mr. de Winter's dead wife, Rebecca. She convinces the girl that Rebecca was perfect, beautiful, that the husband will never love her the way he did his first wife. It's all Rebecca, Rebecca, Rebecca. The housekeeper even convinces the girl she should just give up and jump out a window, and then—

"Good book?" Dad interrupted.

Irritated, I refused to take my eyes off the page. "It's not *No Shirt, No Pulse, No Problem.*"

"You know you're not supposed to read my stuff. All those corpses, they'll give you nightmares."

I could've reminded him of my long-retired bedtime story, but instead I huffed, "I'm seventeen. Not seven."

He sighed. "So you are. Sometimes, Immy, I wish I could go back. Be your age again."

"Cool. You can go to high school tomorrow, and I'll sit around in my underwear and write all day."

Dad laughed dryly. "Someday you'll appreciate it. You'll look back and remember when all these doors were open to you. You just wait and see. You get older, and you make your choices, and one by one the doors shut."

I closed *Rebecca*. Dad didn't usually talk this way. I rolled away on my side, awkward, and cramped from reading on my stomach, and annoyed. I couldn't see what was so great about being my age anyway. I spent every morning in the bathroom cataloguing what I didn't like about myself, I had crushes on boys who had no use for me, and I had friends I wasn't even sure I liked half the time. "Why did you really let me skip today?"

I felt him stand, sand shifting beneath the blanket to fill the empty space he'd left behind. "Oh, I don't know. Sometimes I just . . . wish we had more time."

I craned my neck over my shoulder to watch him walk down the beach, his sneakers crunching shells and seaweed strands, his head down against the wind.

By the time I picked up my book again, the sun had ducked behind the clouds, and I was colder than before. I tucked myself deeper into my jacket, pressed my sunglasses into my nose, and shut my eyes.

I woke up stiff to Dad shaking my shoulder, saying, "Immy, we have to head out. Lindy will wonder where we are." I could tell it was late by the slant of the sun on the sand, the blue shadows that stretched behind us like our own private pools of water. There was no time to grab food in town—we'd barely beat Lindy home from work, even if we sped—so we stopped at a McDonald's for fries to fill us up until dinner. Just before pulling out of the drive-through and back onto the highway, Dad turned off the engine, twisted in his seat, and looked me in the eyes.

"I love you, *bou bui*." The Cantonese word for "darling" or "treasure," which Dad hadn't called me in years and years, not since Ma Ma Scott was around, and I always thought it was for my Chinese grandmother's benefit.

"Yeah, okay," I answered, embarrassed. "I love you too and whatever."

"And whatever." He sniffed.

Avoiding my stepmother's eyes, I tell most of this to Officer Griffin.

"So that's that," Lindy says. "We went to bed last night, and when I got up this morning he wasn't here, and he'd left everything behind. When he never came back, I called you all."

"Good, good." As Officer Griffin writes, she twirls a stray piece of brown hair around one finger. It's funny because dozens of girls in my grade do the same, and absolutely nothing else about Officer Griffin is "girlie." Except for a few escaped strands, her hair is scraped into a hard little knot at the back of her skull. Her eyebrows are wild, her shoulders square, her skin pink and rough. I wonder who her daughter is. Sugarbrook is small enough that I might know her; in fact, there's an Ashley Griffin in a few of my AP classes, a supernaturally pretty senior who wears body glitter and purple and gold hair chalk, our school colors, to soccer games with the rest of the popular girls. I've never seen Officer Griffin at a game, but maybe Ashley is embarrassed by her mother. I guess daughters sometimes are.

Sitting across from the officer, Lindy looks her opposite in every way. Even though it's late at night and we're in our own home, diamonds hang from her earlobes on thin chains, the crystals twinkling against her sculpted blond hair. Instead of a bathrobe or a sweater she has a cape wrapped around herself, a white wool thing with pink silk lining. When she stands and stretches, the silk yawns inside her sleeves like the tongue of a snow-white animal. Officer Griffin's fuzzy coat hangs gracelessly over her chair back. This is a town of Nikes and North Face, and Lindy clips around it in heels and Burberry.

She tilts the coffeepot into her mug. When nothing drips out, she sighs and sets it in the sink. "Immy, it's late, and you have school tomorrow."

Officer Griffin snaps her book shut. "You're right about that. But this is good, a good place to start. You think of anything else, Lindy, you give us a call. You too, Imogene."

I nod, slump out of the kitchen, and pretend to climb the stairs to my bedroom. Instead I stop on the landing and drop silently to the carpet to listen in. There's the *clank* of Lindy dumping the rest of the cups in the sink, and then in a low voice she asks, "How does this work now? I mean, what can we expect from the police?" She sounds calm, but of course it's her job to stay composed.

"First off, you did the right thing, calling us." Officer Griffin is trying to keep quiet, but hers is the brassy kind of Bostonian voice that carries. "Now, we got Mr. Scott's pictures, and a list of his friends, and his credit card number, though we know he left his card with you. The fact that he didn't take out a whole bunch of money is good—means he's probably not planning on staying gone too long. I'll get this info out to everyone on patrol, put in a report to NCIC—that's the National Crime Information Center. In the meantime, keep his cell phone with you in case he calls in, or somebody who knows something calls.

"But you have to understand, it doesn't look like foul play. Your husband doesn't have any serious health problems. I know you got some concerns about his mental state, but the fact that he planned for this shows he's at least in control of his faculties, you know? We'll look into this. But . . . it isn't always a crime to go missing. We do find him, we'll take it from there. Just do us a favor:

you and your stepdaughter sit tight. You think of anyone who might know anything, let us know. But don't
go investigating on your own. That won't help anyone."

"I understand."

"Just one more question before I go, Mrs. Scott.
Today being what it is—does that mean anything special to you? Besides, you know, the roses-and-candies
rigmarole?"

"I don't think so. Sometimes Josh remembers,
sometimes he's working on a book and he doesn't. My
husband . . . isn't always a Valentine's Day sort of person."

Lindy thanks Officer Griffin and in the shuffle of
her leaving, I creep the rest of the way into my room,
quickly shuck off my jeans, and lie on my bed in the
dark. Lindy won't believe I'm asleep already, not even
close, but she'll read the signs. She'll know better than
to talk to me.

Sure enough, after she climbs the stairs, her shadow
pauses outside my bedroom door for only a moment
before the hall light clicks off and her footsteps carry
her away to her own room.

I give it a minute, then ease open the drawer of my
nightstand, where I find the subject of my second half
truth. It's not that I lied to Officer Griffin; I only left
out the part of the story that wouldn't mean anything

to her, and she'd think I was crazy if I told her what it meant to me. So how could it possibly help us?

Carefully, carefully, I lift out a perfect half of a fist-size gray stone, left here by Dad in the night. It must have been; it was here when I got up this morning, no note or anything, just the stone heart I've never been allowed to hold and haven't seen in five or six years—not since Dad met Lindy, at least. I cup the rock close to my nose in the blue-black dark. Even now, the crystals glitter faintly in the starlight through my curtains.

Down the hall Lindy stirs loudly in the big bedroom—banging around in her closet, maybe, or searching my dad's for clues. While I wait for her to go to sleep I clutch the stone to my chest, curled up around my secret like an oyster around a pearl.

crime scenes and rib spreaders. He joked it'd make me creepy, besides; a pale little kid who reads books about a morgue could turn into a pale teenager who sets death traps for squirrels and weaves their delicate matchstick bones into friendship bracelets. Which, all right, maybe I'm not a homecoming queen, but I've never once set a death trap for anything.

None of his protests worked. I was nine when I read his very first novel, *A Time to Chill*. I didn't understand every four-syllable word or the science of cadavers, and did my best to skip over the naked parts (dead-naked, not sex-naked), but I was hooked. Captivated. When at last he wised up, he brought me kid books by the paper-bagful. Parentally acceptable stuff like *From the Mixed-Up Files of Mrs. Basil E. Frankweiler*. Everything by Caroline B. Cooney. The stiff, yellow-spined Nancy Drews. I didn't enjoy the trashy teenage-thriller stuff so much. Girls my age now (who seemed so old then) hiding in dark corners in skimpy summer dresses. Or running down an alley with their blond hair streaming. Or caught in a pair of headlights on a dark road by some unseen vehicle. They were always scared shitless, those girls on the covers. And they hardly ever solved their own mysteries. What happened was the big bad guy would find the girl before the girl found him, then chase her around a Florida swamp for a while until an alligator ate him from behind at the last possible second. But I read those books anyway, and picked up the next before the "Oh, come on" had rolled off my tongue. Soon enough I went back to the adult stuff, the classics I like best with brooding detectives and grisly murders and grown women, but sometimes I still read the old books, visit those silly girls on dark roads.

There's just something about a mystery. You've got this question rattling around your head, so all-consuming that there's hardly room for anything else. What's Moriarty up to now? Who's the devil in a blue dress? What *is* the secret of the old clock? But the whole time, you have faith you'll have your answer by the last page.

No, more than faith. Before she was my stepmother, Lindy said in one of our few sessions together that faith is a special thing that only exists where there isn't any proof. Faith was how thirteen-year-old me had dealt with my dad flopping through life like a fish onshore for the few months prior, one of the roughest bad times he'd been through.

Faith has never been my forte. Even Miles Faye, the star of Dad's books, doesn't operate on it; throughout the novels, the handsome forensic pathologist is all about the facts, always muttering to himself, "What do you *know*, Miles?" Right now, I could fill my own book with what I *don't* know about Dad. I have the stone heart, and a theory that even I'll admit sounds crazy, but few hard facts.

But that's okay. Because in mysteries, if nothing else you *know* that no matter how weird or dark or hopeless things get, one way or another it'll all be right by the end.

After a long and silent hour, by which time I'm sure Lindy's in bed for good, I leave my room and pad barefoot down to Dad's office. He and I made a deal that he'd never rifle through my bedroom looking for weed or notes from boys or squirrel bones, and I'd never snoop in his office, where he keeps his scribbled notes and half-birthed books and who knows what else. I doubt he'd care if I snuck around in his bedroom (Lindy absolutely *would* care) but his office is his private space.

Still, didn't he invite me in by leaving our stone for me to find?

The summer before I started high school, Dad took me out for pizza to let me know he was dating our brand-new family therapist. He'd never brought a woman home before because he loved me and he loved us, and I was all he needed. But now that I was old enough, maybe I could understand that he sometimes felt . . . "isolated," he had said. He never said lonely, was always really careful with the L-word.

I concentrated on building a breadstick bridge across my salad bowl and asked, "Why are you telling me this, anyway?"

He reached over the pizza and patted my hand. "Because you have big shoulders. You know what that means?"

I didn't then, but maybe now I do.

I turn the knob to Dad's office, putting my weight on it as I push the door open so the warped edge won't scrape the top of the frame. Usually it's locked. Lindy and Officer Griffin must've opened it; I know there's a spare key hidden in the decade-old plastic cactus on the kitchen windowsill. Inside it's dark. The streetlights outside filter through the horizontal blinds, painting pale bars on the carpet. It's a little creepy. Not that I'm afraid of the dark or anything pathetic, but for some reason when it's late at night or ungodly early, this house I've lived in all my life doesn't feel . . . quite like mine. Like the hallways are longer, the furniture just to the left of where I remember it, the people in the pictures slightly unfamiliar.

When I breathe deeply, the sweet-spicy clove smell of Djarum Black cigarettes fills the room. Dad's favorite, a kind of pretentious habit he picked up when he quit his very practical job and sat down to type his first book. To Lindy's dismay, he inhales them by the carton every few years when he's truly, especially stressed, and even though he swears he sticks his head out the window to smoke, the smell clings.

I trail my fingers along his desk, cluttered with all the stuff you'd expect. Coffee mugs crammed with pens. Printed pages in a dozen stacks with scribbles that'd be indecipherable to anyone but Dad. His favorite paperweight, which I bought him on a field trip to the New England Aquarium: a plastic mermaid floating in sleek blue glass. His laptop, which Lindy has combed through and Officer Griffin has briefly perused. Neither of them found a document titled "*Where I Am* by Joshua Scott." Nor did they find a roadmap marked with a big red X in his desk drawers. I open them anyway to double-check, and find only tins of mints and Dunkin' Donuts receipts and a Rubik's Cube, unsolved.

On the bookshelf, I see what I really came in for. I pull out *A Time to Chill,* the first book in the row of Dad's novels. On the dedication page, I find the familiar words: "To Sidonie, with all my love." The rest of Dad's stuff is dedicated to me or, in books published after Lindy came along, to "my best girls."

In the very back where the author's headshot should go, there is instead a picture of my mother holding me in her hospital room at Good Shepherd (which gives the impression that Joshua Scott is either a small woman with a masculine name, or a baby). She's in an armchair, limp-haired and haggard and blurred with sweat. She cradles pink newborn me in her arms, resting against a still-ballooned stomach under her hospital gown. I think she looks happy. I mean, it's not the most flattering picture; maybe that's why she never wanted Dad to take another. There aren't many pictures of me and my mother. Which seems crazy; you can't spend five minutes on Facebook without stumbling into two hundred photos of some older cousin's kid eating Cheerios. Then again, she left when I was two. All my baby pictures fit in a polka-dot child's album, and my mother must've snapped most of them, because she's not in them. When she does show up in shots, she's a white pair of hands steadying me as I climb into a laundry basket, or she's the hem of a skirt, a socked foot, a bent knee, or the nut-brown tips of her dangling hair.

These flashes in the corners of photos are all I have. Aside from the story of her leaving, Dad never talked about my mother. "That's all in the past," he said whenever I asked. But we read Faulkner in AP English last fall, and I know Dad has a bunch of him on the shelf between Terence Faherty and Gillian Flynn. So I think he should know better that the past isn't dead . . . or however that old quote goes.

I shove back Dad's battered rolling chair from the

desk and settle down in the groove that's almost warm, then start up his laptop. It's a sleek black machine that I'm not supposed to touch, but have on rare occasions. The password—*Faye4321*—has always been scribbled on a sticky note under his mouse pad. Not his most cunning maneuver.

The laptop pings to life, too loud in the silent house, the screen unnaturally bright in the dark office. After I punch in the password, his background picture materializes, some old painting of fishermen in a boat.

A man of complicated tastes, my dad.

I click search on the start menu and look for "Sidonie Scott" in all documents, then in all files and folders and then, desperately, in pictures and videos. "Sidonie" turns up nothing either, so I open an internet window and Google "Sidonie Scott," not for the first time. Not for the fiftieth time either. No dice. I've tried to use Google-fu to find out more about my mother than the next-to-nothing my dad's been willing to tell me. But there's no Sidonie Scott on Facebook, or LinkedIn, or in the online White Pages. No one's written a single news article about a Sidonie Scott who could possibly be my mother. And it's not like it's a common name. As far as I can tell, she's nowhere.

Of course, other than her name (and not even her maiden name, at that) I don't have much to go on. Dad hasn't heard from her since the divorce papers, filed through a lawyer who kept her location a secret. After that, Ma Ma Scott left my resilient Scottish grandfather alone in Maine for a few years to help Dad look after me. This I remember in a fuzzy slideshow of dress-up games and PB&J lunches and Dad staggering in from work and crushing me to him as if he hadn't expected to find me at home waiting.

So we weren't always the happiest family in Happy Town. But I wasn't a gloomy kid or, contrary to Dad's predictions, a creepy kid, and life wasn't so bad. The worst that happened in an average day was my dad forgot to buy hot-dog buns because he was wrapped up in writing *Vital Signs*, so we used folded white bread like a pair of losers. Just sometimes, usually at night, and especially when Dad was going through one of his bad times, there was this thing, a dumb hungry animal in my chest. And I didn't know what to call it, but I knew that it was my mother. My dad must've felt it too. Otherwise he wouldn't have had the bad times, would he? At least, that was my theory.

On a whim I Google "Joshua Scott." The usual turns up: "Joshua Scott is the author of a series of medical mystery novels following forensic pathologist Dr. Miles Faye," yada yada. I scroll through, but there's nothing about Joshua Scott disappearing. How long will that last?

I push myself back from the desk and hug the copy of *A Time to Chill*. I need to think. No, I need to think like Dad. How hard can it be to find him when I've been reading his mysteries since I was a kid? He even left a clue for me especially. The stone heart won't be in Officer Griffin's missing persons report. But then, I'm not sure Dad is missing. I mean, he's clearly not here, but giving me the heart like this, it can't be meaningless. He wouldn't ditch me for any old reason. He must be searching for something. Or, considering what he left behind, for *someone*. And searching isn't missing.

Well, I can search too.

I've even got an idea where to start. Whenever I'm trying to find a lost object—a favorite mystery, a very un-favorite textbook, my cell phone, a sneaker—Lindy's well-meaning and unoriginal advice is: "Figure out where you last had it, and that's where you should start looking."

I don't remember my mom, but the picture in back of this book is my proof that she was real, that she was a whole person who once held me. And if that's the case, then maybe Good Shepherd is where I truly had her last.

FOUR

While Mr. McCormick fiddles with the volume on *Love's Labour's Lost*—not the play, but the musical where Alicia Silverstone's Princess of France speaks with nearly the same accent as Cher—I reach across the aisle and poke Jessa Price with my pencil eraser.

It takes a few pokes to get her attention. Jessa's face is forever blue-lit by the screen of an iSomething. iPod, iPad, iPhone, doesn't matter. She rotates between them by the minute. Now she's peeking at her iPhone below the lip of her desk, texting Jeremy White. I know it's him because her texts are heavily sprinkled with winky-face emoticons. I prod her once more.

"What?" she huffs.

"Want to go into Boston this weekend?"

She looks up at last, big blue eyes surfacing to meet mine. "When?"

"Hmm," I pretend to ponder. "When's your mom working? Can she give us a ride?"

Frowning, Jessa sweeps her hair behind her ear and over one shoulder. It's the rich red-blond of apple cider and she touches it all the time, the same way Dad pats his pockets to make sure he's got everything he needs. It's no secret that she's gorgeous. She knows she's beautiful the way I know yellow and blue make green. Some girls don't like that. Liz Bash sneers about her in the second-floor bathroom and says she's one of *those* girls (like there's only two kinds of girls, and you're one of *those* or you aren't). I'm not exactly Jessa's white knight, but I don't see the point in begrudging her looks. I'm fine, possibly cute from certain angles and under the right circumstances and with enough work, but sometimes I think I'd eat live spiders and roll in rotten fruit to see what Jessa sees in the mirror, just for a day.

"Why can't we take your car?" she asks.

"I need to bring it to the garage for the weekend. Something's up with the starter." This is a half truth, as there have been a few shaky starts recently. What follows is the total lie: "I really want to go *shopping*." I slip a little whine in my voice.

"Fine, I'll text Mom and find out." She hardly bothers to hide her phone, but she won't get caught. Mr. McCormick's done fussing with the DVD player and has retreated to his desk, surrounded by copies of Bram Stoker's *Dracula* and stacks of everyone's essay but mine (Lindy went with "a family matter" in her note). Anyway, it's Friday, and the last Friday before February break. Not a teacher at Sugarbrook High has their head in the game, hence Alicia Silverstone. In history next period, I'm betting we'll watch a History Channel documentary on Nazis.

This is good. It gives me time to plan. I'd go into the city alone if I could. Technically, Jessa and I are best friends. We grew up in each other's houses. Shared teething rings, then sleeping bags, then issues of *Vogue*. A few years ago we learned about mutualism in biology; how a certain kind of shrimp will drill a sandy home in the seafloor, and in will move a goby fish alongside it. Seems generous, but the shrimp is mostly blind and counts on the little bug-eyed fish to keep watch, and warn it with the flailing of its body if a bigger fish approaches. I hang out over at Jessa's house and let her copy my English homework and sometimes math, which I secretly love because it's just like a puzzle written in code. And while I'm there, Jessa polishes up my hopeless art assignments or paints my nails. Meanwhile I get to gaze at her big brother, Chad, who lives in their giant luxury basement and goes to college, and who I've had a lingering and unrequited crush on since fifth grade. I guess that makes me the goby fish?

Maybe that all sounds bad. *Machiavellian,* Mr. McCormick would say. Maybe it's just honest. But I'm counting on Jessa for three reasons:

1. She doesn't have a car, never even got her license, and depends on Chad or her parents or her boyfriends to drive her anywhere.

2. She will never turn down a suggestion to shop on Newbury Street, though I can barely afford the cupcakes.

3. Most important, Dr. Van Tassel—Jessa's mom, who is all about girl power, and doctors under her maiden name—works at Good Shepherd Hospital. I know for a fact she usually has second shift on Saturdays. And it's her I really need.

While I'm waiting for an answer I slide my hand into the front pocket of the faux-leather satchel at my feet—a present from Dad for my seventeenth birthday—and rasp my fingers against the rough outside of the stone. Whenever I feel myself start to panic because Dad's been missing for two days now, I think of the stone and repeat to myself that he's searching. He's searching. He's searching. I wanted to stay home today and start my own search, but Lindy wouldn't let me, said I'd already missed on Tuesday and, in situations like these, normalcy is the best policy. Whatever she means by that. School won't be normal for long, not once word gets out.

As far as I can tell, none of my classmates know Dad's gone. Yet. I spent most of chemistry eyeing Ashley Griffin, who revealed nothing. No sympathetic half smiles, no gossiping behind her purple-painted nails. Of course, she might not even be Officer Griffin's daughter, but she's still the type who knows everything before everyone else. I don't think I've ever seen her surprised, not by the box of Plan B that tumbled out of Dominique Melcher's backpack during study hall or Josh Lopez's brother's second DUI. Girls like Ashley Griffin are the mouth of the river of gossip at Sugarbrook High, and the rest of us try not to sink in the current. Say what you will about Jessa (and you can say a lot), but she doesn't blab secrets.

Not that I plan to tell her about Dad. I don't plan to tell anyone. I'm not embarrassed or anything—I know Dad must have a good reason for skipping out in the night—it's just that nothing anyone comes up with will be the truth. They'll say he ran out on us, or that his murdered body is floating listlessly down the Mystic River. False and false. I don't want anyone to think of my dad that way.

I flinch as a pencil flips past my face and clatters against the frosted windowpane to my left. Katie Rodriguez and Liz Bash giggle behind me, but Mr. McCormick doesn't look up. I turn on Jessa, who grins unapologetically.

"Mom's working at three tomorrow. She'll drive us in, but we have to, like, get my brother to pick us up after."

I give her a thumbs-up and sit back, my eyes on the TV screen to extricate myself from conversation. When the bell rings, Jessa kicks my shin a little too roughly with one red Converse, says "Call you later, Im," and walks off without looking up from her phone. Her sequined hoodie winks under the fluorescents and her tight jeans ripple like a second skin. Thus goes my great hope.

After school lets out at three, it's a fight to get out the door. February break has made everyone a little manic, and I thread through the crowd with my head down, between the senior boys hurtling themselves against lockers, the band kids slinging around black clarinet cases, the slow-moving art kids with ear gauges the size of quarters. When I make it to the parking lot, I watch Oriel Perotta plow right over the island, running down winter-dead grass, cutting through the dinky skate park the school put up to "keep kids out of trouble." By "trouble" I guess they mean getting high outside the Burger King on Elm Street, the most likely mischief for Sugarbrook students. Ours is one of two small high schools in town—the other is J. Jefferson Agricultural High, for the aggies from the tobacco farms and cranberry bogs just west of us.

This place would show up under a "Middle-of-the-Road Small Town, USA" Google search. Just down the street from school is the Patty Linden Memorial Park, with a shabby stone fountain where the graduating class dumps laundry detergent every June so it foams over the lawn. Around the park, half of the brick one-story businesses are either on the brink or closed for good. Tommy's Bicycles hasn't had a new bike in the window in five years. Larissa's Hair on Main hasn't replaced a wig since the nineties, it's rumored. Jamison's Bakery shuttered when Mrs. Jamison ran off with a police officer from Malden, and is still for sale four years later. I guess there used to be a big electronics company in Sugarbrook, but a decade ago it moved to Boston. Now almost everyone goes to the city to work. A lot of people take the train out of Sugarbrook Station. In fact, it seems like half of Sugarbrook works at Good Shepherd, like Dr. Van Tassel. It's just one of those towns.

Once I steer clear of the businesses and the main streets clogged with students' cars, it's easy moving through the streets. As I drive east from the middle-class end to the rich-kid end, the pools and trampolines multiply, blocked in by iron gates instead of rough fences. Dad and Lindy and I live right in the middle on Cedar Lane. Down the street and with a considerably bigger fence is the Prices' house. When we were young, Ma Ma Scott and Jessa's nanny shoved us together, nurturing a friendship based on our mutual smallness and nearness to each other. That's all little girls need to be buddies. They don't even really need to like each other. So back then Jessa and I were friends because, well, there we were, and now we're friends because we were friends back then. Simple math.

I rattle into the driveway of my pale green house at 42 Cedar Lane and am surprised to find Lindy on the porch glider. She's wrapped in her cape and rocking slowly with her heels crossed. Maybe it's the way she hunches down as the wind tugs at her, or the lack of hairspray in her frazzled yellow hair, but all at once I feel worse for her than myself. She doesn't deserve to be totally in the dark. Maybe it's selfish to keep my clue and my theory to myself. I've got a message from Dad to hang on to; Lindy's got nothing.

"What are you doing?" I ask as I climb the porch steps.

"I made this flier on the computer," she says. "I was thinking of printing out a bunch of them, dropping them off at the grocery store and the mall."

I glance briefly at the paper in her lap and see Dad's bubble-pipe headshot from *No Shirt, No Pulse, No Problem*, and in bold font just below, the caption: MISS-ING. *Jesus*, I think, sick at the thought of incoming gossip, and look away without reading the rest. Instead, I pick at a loose thread on the glider seat, patterned with squiggly ivy vines. "How will that help? It's not like Dad got lost in the produce aisle."

She cups her hand around her chin and drums her fingers against her lips while she looks at me sideways. "I'm exploring all of our avenues," she says evenly.

"Explore a different avenue," I snipe. "Stake out a few places before you put a poster up in Wetzel's Pret-zels." I'm probably picking a fight to squash this twist of guilt on my dad's behalf.

To my great surprise, Lindy nods. "That seems rea-sonable. All right, where shall we start?"

I frown, wondering what kind of trap I'm walking into. "Like, together?"

"Sure. We won't get in anybody's way. But I'd like to spend some time with you, and if you feel like taking a drive, we can keep our eyes open as we go, can't we?"

"I guess. . . ."

"Okay then." She claps her hands, her gold watch jangling around her slim wrist. "What if we head out to that beach you both love? Seems like a good place to start. We could go right now, in fact. What do you say?"

The cops already did a sweep of Victory Island this morning; Lindy told me so when I checked in during lunch. But I can use the ride to sniff out scraps of information Lindy may have on Sidonie Scott. Besides, my only argument against it is my natural aversion to alone time with Lindy. And I can't tell her that. She's okay, for a stepmother. I don't know if any thirteen-year-old would be psyched to share their dad and their bathroom with a new woman. But even if Lindy and I never did the whole hair-braiding, chick-flick-watching, homemade-cookies thing, she could've been worse. She left her fancy Boston practice and joined a smaller clinic in Framingham just so she could break the rules and be with Dad, so I guess she loves him. And if it was weird to have this therapist we'd been seeing suddenly walking around my house in her silk pajamas, at least she didn't try to smother me or anything. She said I was a "partner in the family," and never treated me like a pain, or the price of marrying

Dad, or some pathetic little half orphan.

So yeah, it could've been worse, for sure.

I don't know what's gotten into Lindy, or what her angle is. But maybe it doesn't matter. Maybe this is just another case of mutualism.

Crawling through rush hour traffic, Lindy and I retrace Wednesday's route to the island. While bogged down on I-95, she keeps our conversation bland and safe:

"How's that English paper coming along?"

"It's okay. I got an extension."

"Did you score the defense attorney spot in mock trial?"

"Don't know yet."

"How many volunteer hours are you up to?"

"Don't know. Twenty? Twenty-two?"

"That hamper of your whites in the laundry room— are you waiting for a special occasion to wash them?"

"Not particularly."

I'm pleasantly surprised by her benign questions. What Lindy really likes is some good self-reflection. It's the therapist in her, which dozes but never truly slumbers. If I leave my late-night cheese and crackers and cold chicken and ice cream dishes in the sink? We have a talk about pride, and whether my lack of pride in my surroundings signals a lack of pride in myself. If I get a B-minus on a calculus test? We have a talk about my potential, and how my intelligence is a responsibility, and requires responsible choices, and what can we do to nurture said responsibility?

I count myself lucky and, in the breaths between answers, formulate my own questions for the drive back.

The beach, when we reach it at last, is even colder today. The wind whips brutally through the dunes, and with every step Lindy's boot heels sink into the sand like golf tees.

The first time I remember coming here, it was one of the hottest nights in a legendarily hot summer. Dad told me so. A thunderstorm had knocked the power out and killed our air conditioner hours before, turned our house into a miserable, sticky swamp. In the middle of the night, after the storm blew past us, Dad came into my bedroom, where I was sweating through My Little Pony pajamas. He drove us to the coast. I don't know how he found our particular beach, if he just went eastward until he couldn't anymore, but I do know it was right around the Fourth of July, because I watched from the highway as amateur fireworks popped off above the cities. We walked barefoot through the still-warm sand. Lightning flashed in the distance over the ocean, and behind us, fireworks bloomed over Newburyport, so the whole sky was lit up in turns. It's the first time I remember my little child-brain formulating the words I'd repeat to myself, often and forcefully: *We are enough.*

Silently, Lindy and I trudge a little ways up the beach, chins tucked into our collars. I don't think either of us expects to find Dad huddled over a driftwood bonfire.

When sunset dusts the sky, we drive in circles through the kite shops and themed motels and clam shacks. We park pointlessly to show Dad's photo inside a used bookshop he loves, and a gallery of wood carvings where he's always threatening to buy something. As if Dad only stepped out to pick up a half-price paperback or a leaping salmon totem pole for the scraggly flowerbed in our front yard.

"It was a long shot," Lindy says, and sighs as we turn and head for home. I agree; this place is ours, mine and Dad's, so I hardly think the trail to my mother winds through the Victory Island Soap Emporium. Lindy doesn't seem dejected, though. I think she spent more time side-eyeing me than scanning the streets out her window.

Still, I give it a little time before I break the silence. "So, did Dad ever tell you any stories? From before?"

"Before?" She takes the entrance ramp for the turnpike.

"I don't know. Before . . . you."

"You mean, did he tell me about your childhood?"

"Or before that."

She wipes her wind-snarled hair out of her face. "What specifically are you asking me, Immy?"

I kick at the sandy floor mat below my boots. Stupid therapy-communication-speak. "Did he ever tell you about, like, my mother?"

Her perfectly manicured and moisturized hands tighten slightly around the wheel. "Your father has never been very effusive about that relationship."

"Yeah, I know he isn't *effusive*. I'm just asking . . ." The next words are a little painful to speak aloud, like needling out a splinter. "Did he tell you stuff about her he wouldn't tell me? In sessions or anything?"

"No," she says slowly. "Only that your mother left when you were two, and the divorce was finalized shortly after. And that your mother had her problems, as we all do. He didn't talk about them, and it would be irresponsible of me to speculate." Lindy glances over at me. "I was always more interested in your father's history."

"But did my mom ever—"

"I wanted to talk to you about something, Immy," she cuts me off, which is not like her. "I want to talk to you about your dad. About what's been going on around here. I don't know how much you've picked up on. . . ."

"Well, I've picked up on the fact that he's *not* here."

"I mean before that. You know your dad's had some real trouble in the past."

A horn honks through the quiet in the car, and Lindy flicks on the blinker, glides into the slow lane. I can feel this horrible, queasy seed sprouting in my stomach.

"That was a long time ago," I finally answer.

"Not so very long. Your father . . . he's had a hard time of it. Periodically. He was going through a stretch of it when I met him." She looks over at me, suddenly flustered. "Of course, you remember, because you were there. He's been battling this in therapy, and he takes his medication. And he has us. You know how much he loves you."

"That's not what's happening," I say coldly.

"Immy, wherever he's gone, he left his medication behind." She lifts a hand from the wheel and lays it atop my own, which I've fisted into the seat without noticing. "This is not his fault. This is not our fault."

"You think he's crazy?"

"Bipolar disorder is a condition, Immy. You know better than that. It's medical, it isn't—"

"He's not crazy. I would know." As I yell at her, I flip through the past few months, sift through moments of my dad. Were there any of the old signs from the bad times? That Sunday afternoon I came home to find him on the couch at three p.m.—was he napping? Staring listlessly at the ceiling? Did I have to call his name a bunch of times before he heard? Was his voice slow and slightly blurry when he answered, as if fighting up through water to reach the air? And that other night, was he wandering the halls at three a.m., or mumbling to himself behind locked bathroom doors? I think of the beach. He was a little different on the beach . . . but no. I would've noticed if he was changing. Changing back. He's been fine for years. He's perfectly fine.

"Dad didn't go off because he's *sad*. He would never . . . You don't know what you're . . ."

"I'm not trying to hurt you, Immy. I just don't want to keep anything from you. Not about your dad." She sighs again and squints into the mirror. "We're in this together."

I turn and see big tears bunched in the corners of her eyes. Also very un-Lindy-like.

"Whatever," I mutter, blinking wetly. I crank on the radio, not caring enough to switch the station when an NPR drone fusses over the tech boom in California.

Dad's searching. I have the stone heart to prove it. He didn't leave it for Lindy because she doesn't know him like I do. I've had Dad for seventeen years. They've been together barely four. She wouldn't know where to look for him, how to find him. I realize now that Lindy never expected anything to come of Victory Island; she drove us two and a half hours round-trip to trap me and ask me about my *feelings*. Which proves that, unlike me, she has no idea which questions to ask. If Dad had left the heart in *her* dresser drawer, she wouldn't have the faintest clue what it meant. She wouldn't listen if I told her.

We ride home without another word until Lindy pulls back into our driveway, and so gently it's obnoxious, says, "Immy, if there's anything you ever need to talk about—"

"Nope. I'm good. I'm fine," I say briskly. "In fact, I'm going shopping with Jessa tomorrow."

Lindy looks over at me, surprised. "Oh. Okay. I think that's a good idea."

"I'm not doing it because it's a good idea."

She holds her hands up in surrender. Her fancy gold watch slips down her wrist, spinning around her perfectly tanned and sculpted arm. Who is this person, I wonder, this woman who lived a whole life before I knew her? Then, before I can feel sorry for my stepmother, I gather up my bag and hurry from the car. I slam the front door and shut Lindy out behind me.

What do I need her for when I've got big shoulders?

FIVE

As I slide across the backseat of Dr. Van Tassel's cherry-red Solstice early Saturday afternoon, she blasts me with a big smile in the rearview mirror and says, "Imogene, honey, how are you? How wonderful to see you!"

This is how I find out she knows exactly what's going on. Dr. Van Tassel is nice, but not gushingly, welcome-to-my-Solstice nice.

"I'm good, Dr. Van Tassel. How are you?"

Jessa cranks around in her seat to grin at me. "She's *great*. Dad came back from France last night and brought super-fancy champagne, and guess who's been guzzling it since?"

Dr. Van Tassel swats at her daughter's shoulder, hidden under glossy red-gold hair that matches her own, though hers is chopped short around her plump chin. "That was a mimosa, and it's a breakfast drink." She eyes me again in the mirror. "And it was two hours ago."

"Mmkay, Dr. Denial." Jessa snickers.

Dr. Van Tassel adjusts her glasses—huge, round, red frames like twin stop signs. Jessa thinks they're hipster-chic, but Dr. Van Tassel doesn't care about that. She doesn't know the difference between pearl gray and heather gray, between boot-cut and straight-leg trousers, not the way Lindy does. Her walk-in closet is only a quarter filled, and mostly with jeans, T-shirts, and patterned scrubs. And while their house is perfectly decorated by a professional, all chrome and leather, slick wall sculptures, it's only because Dr. Van Tassel had no desire to decorate herself, which seems the best reason to do a dumb thing like hiring an interior designer.

"How are things, Immy? How's school? It's been a little while, hasn't it?" Translation: I know your dad is missing.

"School's good."

"That's wonderful. And how's your stepmother?" Translation: I know your dad is missing.

"She's good too."

"Wonderful. I'm so glad to hear it, honey."

Translation: I know your dad is missing, you poor, poor unfortunate waif.

The ride into the city isn't too long. After half an hour on the highway, the skyscrapers of downtown Boston rear up in front of us, then the brownstones. On the west side off the highway, the sun catches and halos the coppery glass complex of Good Shepherd Hospital. Not the biggest hospital in town, but it is the shiniest. "Okay, girls," Dr. Van Tassel says as she pulls into the employee parking lot. "You have everything? T passes? Jessa, you have your cell phone?" It's obvious she does; it's still in front of her face.

"Actually, Dr. Van Tassel, do you think it'd be okay if I talked to you inside? For a minute?"

Jessa looks up. "What? Why?"

Dr. Van Tassel's eyes meet mine in the mirror, and I give my best look of secret sadness. Translation: I am a poor, poor unfortunate waif whose dad is missing. "Right. Okay, honey. Sure thing."

"Just for a minute."

"Of course, Imogene, of course."

"Seriously? Aren't we shopping?"

Dr. Van Tassel grits her teeth. "How about you hang out in the waiting room for a bit, Jessa?"

Jessa sighs. "What am I supposed to do in a hospital?" Then she pulls out her phone and plays Fruit Ninja while we walk. I'm shocked her thumbs aren't worn down to nubs.

The ER entrance by the ambulance bay is dotted with squat, frosted shrubbery. A cluster of hospital workers smokes off the path, arms crossed against the wind that tugs at their scrubs and white coats. In the waiting room, the plastic chairs are half-full, though no one seems on the verge of death. A middle-aged woman in a stained sweater cradles her bandaged left hand and blinks at the television mounted to the wall, while a young gray-faced guy hunches down in the corner, sniffling miserably. Jessa grimaces and picks a seat as far across the room from him as possible. Her mom waves to a cop and a paramedic as we pass, and they toast her with Styrofoam cups of coffee.

Dr. Van Tassel's office is on the fourth floor, in the pediatrics department. She sits at her desk and offers me a seat; there are grown-up-size chairs and miniature child-size chairs lined up against a wall papered with crayon and color pencil drawings, and photos of adorable kids in varying shades of sick. I pull over a grown-up chair and sit, cross my legs, then uncross them and grip the sides of the seat.

"Tell me what you want to talk about, Imogene," she says, leaning in across her desk.

After yesterday's debacle with Lindy, I've been

thinking about how to play this smartly. "Okay. Okay, so . . . I was hoping you could tell me how to look at some medical records."

She winces. "You mean your father's? Honey, I don't think that's for you to worry about."

"My mother's, actually." Dr. Van Tassel's eyebrows shoot up over her glasses frames, so I push forward. "I mean, she hasn't been at Good Shepherd since I was born—at least I don't think so—but Dad said you keep the old records around."

This is sort of true, though he never meant to tell me. What he did was write a series of medical mysteries set in Violet Hill Hospital, described as a skyscraper of copper glass and bricks, surrounded by fat shrubbery. When Dad wrote *A Time to Chill*, he'd been away from Good Shepherd for only a year or two, and I'm pretty sure if I were a new writer making up a hospital, I'd use the one I knew by heart. And at Violet Hill Hospital, they moved the old records into the basement. So said handsome forensic pathologist Miles Faye, while investigating a mysterious violent death (spoiler alert: a sleepwalking man clubbed his father-in-law to death, then dumped the old guy in the Charles River when he woke and found a murder most foul). What Miles didn't say was how long they kept the old records for.

"Imogene, that was a long time ago. If the file was

around, you would have to go to the HIS department and get a Release of Information form. The hospital can't release anything without it. After that, it would take two to four weeks for the health records manager to send them to you."

Two to four weeks? My heart sinks into my stomach. Who can wait that long? "But I was hoping maybe you can help me. I mean, I don't need them to send me the files. I can just look at them here. . . ."

Dr. Van Tassel presses her lips together. "If I could help, I would. But I have to tell you, honey, they might not want to release the records. Not if . . . your mother . . . didn't leave you signed authorization. Maybe if you needed them for some reason, a medical concern?" She stares me down until I look away, toward the photos on the wall. "You know, I thought you might want to tell me how you're doing. It can't be easy for you, with your father—"

"I'm sad," I cut in.

She nods. "I think that's understandable. But Lindy says the police are doing everything they can."

"No, I mean I've *been* sad. Lately. Like before my dad . . . went off." In my lap where Dr. Van Tassel can't see, I crack my knuckles. "I have trouble sleeping. I know my mom was . . . sad. Dad told me. So I thought if I could see her records? Maybe it would be helpful."

Dr. Van Tassel's eyes are big and moony. I get it; I sound pathetic. "Are you talking to someone, Imogene?"

"I'm . . . talking to Lindy about it." Yeah, right.

She sighs. "I suppose her medical records might be around. We move the inactive patient's records out after seven years. That's the legal time limit, but we keep them for another decade or so until we shred them. There's a possibility it's here, but I can't promise."

"Okay, so where do you keep them?"

"Imogene. . ." She presses her lips together again, *her* nervous habit. "What you need to do is go to HIS on the second floor and get a form, explain things to them. I can walk you over, if you like."

"No, that's cool." I stand. "I know you have to work. I can find it."

She walks me to her office door anyway, and with the same googly look that makes me feel bad for lying— and hugely uncomfortable, besides—says, "Come and visit us, huh? Have dinner with us? Mike and I are visiting his parents tomorrow night, but maybe Monday?"

"Sure." A quick wave and I duck out, resolutely not looking back, not down the hallway painted with colorful hot-air balloons, not when I reach the elevator, where I punch the down button and wait, though I imagine Dr. Van Tassel's concerned stare drilling through me from behind. Not something I enjoy, but I think it was worth it. Now I know there's a good chance my mom's file is sitting down in the basement still, a toilet for mice and dust mites, and that I can likely get to it even if the HIS office won't help me. And they probably won't. I don't have two to four weeks to burn.

There are two nurses in the elevator, heading for the lobby. I don't want to press *B* until they get off, lest they think I'm going somewhere I shouldn't. When the elevator pings open, there's Jessa, hands in the pockets of her canary-yellow leather jacket, mouth twisting. "I was coming to find you. That took, like, forever. Can we go?"

A cluster of people are walking toward the elevator, so I make a fast, dumb decision. I reach out and pull Jessa into the elevator and punch the button for the basement and *Close Doors*, and we float downward.

"Whoa, whoa, whoa," she protests.

"Just, shh."

When we get to the basement the elevator opens on empty white halls and low ceilings and fluorescent lights.

"We can't be down here. This is where they keep bodies."

"I know." A good thing, because the morgue is in the basement of Violet Hill Hospital as well, and that means I'm on track. "Wait, how do you know?"

"My mom makes me volunteer here a bunch in the summer, remember? Candy-striping and filing and stuff."

"So you'd know where the old records are?"

She pauses. "Why?"

Our feet squeaking softly on the blue-gray tile floor, I'm already tugging her down the hallway so we're not standing in front of the elevator like a pair of morons waiting to be found. It's not like I don't trust her with my secrets. Okay, it is exactly like that, but who do I trust? I mean, there are girls who invite me to their pool parties (which I sometimes attend, though Dad usually helps me brainstorm excuses; some useful, like dentist appointments, some unhelpful, like hair transplants. We're on the same page as far as parties go. Too much to worry about, too many uncontrolled variables). There are girls I sit with in the cafeteria, and I call them all my friends. We talk about our crushes, and when we run out of crushes we make up new ones on the spot. We have petty fights in homeroom so we can feel the warm thrill of making up in history via passed notes. We do the things friends do.

But I have better friends, who I know all about—Daphne du Maurier, Agatha Christie, Caroline B. Cooney, Graham Greene. Is it really so weird to feel closer to them than anyone else? I can count on them, in the end. And of course, I always have my dad.

But now I don't have a choice. We round the corner and I shoulder open the first door, a big closet of cleaning supplies and those yellow mop buckets on wheels. I take a deep breath and go for it. "I'm looking for my mom's old medical records."

Jessa's crystal-blue eyes soften. The Prices never knew my mother—she left before they moved to Massachusetts and to the neighborhood—but of course they know the story. Jessa's known since we were seven and playing kitchen on the plastic stove in her bedroom. It's one of my first memories: rattling plastic eggs around the tiny pink skillets that came with the set. The sun was painting her hair a bright rose gold, much nicer than my uncombed brown mop, and her white dress I was always so jealous of was like a cloud. Jessa's nanny dressed her like a mini pageant queen, while my dad brought me into Walmart and set me free, at which point I learned for myself that a girl could not make her way through kindergarten with fifteen pairs of glitter tights and one bulldog sweater. Anyway, Jessa turned to me in her perfect dress and asked why I only had a dad. I told her very sincerely that my mom was a beautiful astronaut who sometimes had to go to Texas for training. That lasted until Jessa told Dr. Van Tassel my mother was in space . . . or Texas . . . and Dr. Van

Tassel had a talk with Dad.

That night, Dad told me my bedtime story for the very first time.

Twelve years later, Jessa stares at me in the janitor's closet and tugs on her hair. "Im, why? Is this because of your mom, or because your dad's missing?"

I figured her mom would've told her, but still, I feel my cheeks go cold, my fingers, and suck in a breath. "He's not missing."

"So where is he?"

"I'm trying to figure that out. But I need . . . I need . . ." I grab her hand, feeling a weird and unexpected rush of our old play-kitchen love.

"Your mom's records," she finishes. "Want to tell me why?"

I chew my lip.

"No, of course not," she huffs.

"It's just . . . a theory I'm working on."

"Then why don't you just tell the cops, and they can look up the records? We can't get to them without the keys, anyway."

"But *you* know where the keys are. And I have *you*."

She sighs. "Fine. Fine! But this is a dumb idea and we're gonna get caught and my phone's gonna get taken away again, and just wait in the closet, all right? Security checks down here."

"Please come back before someone pukes."

"This place is just storage. Be quiet and you'll be okay." She eases out of the closet, and with a dramatic look left and right, darts away. The door swings shut behind her.

I overturn a mop bucket and sit and wait, which is fine for a few minutes but after a little while, pretty damn creepy, especially when I think of those bodies waiting for transport down some unknown corridor. Miles Faye was never creeped out by bodies, but then, Miles Faye never had to hide in a mop closet, helplessly pinning his hopes on a girl who sometimes texts Levi Cantu dirty pictures when she meant to text them to Jeremy White. And the blue-gray of the floor, which seemed harmless at first, reminds me of corpse lips, mold-spotted fruit, bruises. Maybe Dad was right: too many crime scenes and rib spreaders do make a girl morbid.

As the time passes and I give up on reading cleaning product labels to distract myself, I wonder how it was for my dad when he was down here. What I really want to do—though it's the most likely place to be caught by hospital staff—is sneak down the corridor and look in the morgue, where he spent so many days, where he pried a stone heart out of my grandmother, where he met my mother. Dad once told me this place wasn't good for him; alone except for the bodies, and under fluorescent lighting unpunctured by windows. In the winter he would enter and exit in total darkness. He said he'd forget what faces looked like in daylight for months at a time, and he was happy to be done with that. Who wouldn't be?

Then again, I've caught him in his office with the shades all drawn after fifteen hours of typing and smoking, sometimes with barely a page to show for it. Before Lindy, I always made sure to knock a couple of times during his binges to remind him he wasn't the last man on earth in some Twilight Zone scenario. And I spent those occasional nights and weekends reading, which is definitely not the same as spending it alone.

Thinking about Dad with no immediate plotting to keep me busy, I get this ache in my chest, pressure building up that curls my lungs like wet paper and makes it hard to breathe. Quickly I dig into the pocket of my puffy coat, find the stone, and hold it until the closet door rattles open.

"It's me." Jessa slips inside, twirling a set of keys clipped to a big plastic Minnie Mouse keychain.

"How?" I hadn't realized how little I expected her to succeed until now.

"Mrs. Masciarelli is the health records manager. I help her file and move boxes and stuff in the summer. It's literally the worst. But sometimes it's okay because

Mrs. Masciarelli has this thing. Incompetence? She has to go to the bathroom, like, every twenty minutes, so last summer I would file for twenty minutes and then go see Jake Elroy, who's this really cute eighteen-year-old who had community service."

I roll my finger through the air.

"Anyway, I said I wanted to gossip and brought her a coffee. It sped things up."

"That's devious."

"Says *you*, 007."

I stand and stretch, having cramped up on the mop bucket. I still hate to ask for help, hate *needing* help, but times are desperate. "So . . . where now?"

She holds up the keys. "To the storage room! If anyone sees us, say we're new volunteers."

"And they'll just leave us alone down here?"

"No, they definitely won't."

We've left the closet, rounded exactly one corner, and gone exactly fifteen feet when Jessa's phone jangles in her purse at top volume.

"Turn it off," I whisper, giving her the evil eye.

"Wait one sec." She digs it out and tucks it into her shoulder. "What?" she says into it.

"Turn it off!"

"Oh my god, calm down," she says. "It's my brother." She listens for a minute and then elbows me, totally unnecessary since I'm still staring daggers at her. "Chad says he can only drive us home tonight if we meet him and Jeremy at the Friendly Toast at seven. Want to?"

Perma-crush on Chad notwithstanding, it is impossible to explain how much I don't care. "Just get off the phone, Jessa. Please?"

"We'll see you there," Jessa whispers—a little late for stealth, if you ask me—and turns off the volume on her phone. "Okay, okay. It's off. Happy?" There are locked doors on either side of us. Jessa points out the medical supply room, food supplies, linen storage, the big laundry room where they wash the lab coats and bedsheets and whatever else is bloodied up. "And here"—she sorts through and selects a key with a blue rubber cap, then slots it in a doorknob—"is the file storage. Voilà!" We hurry inside and shut ourselves in the musty dark before Jessa finds the switch. The lights flicker on halfheartedly.

"Shit," I can't help but mutter. Milk crates pale with dust are stacked on shelves around a storage room bigger than our whole basement in Sugarbrook.

"I know, right?" she says. "But it's not that bad. It's sorted by year, and then, like, alphabetically."

I unzip my coat and stuff it in the corner alongside my messenger bag, cleared of schoolwork and all my books but one. "Okay, so I just have to find the box for *S* in 1998." To my surprise, Jessa unzips her own jacket, lays it carefully on top of the only island above the dusty floor—my bag and coat—loops her hair into a loose ponytail, and heads over to the shelves, her skinny black cords swishing against each other as she goes.

"What're you doing?" I ask.

"Baking."

"I was thinking you could be more of a lookout."

"Oh please, hardly anyone comes in here. Not even Mrs. Masciarelli, not without her keys. God, I can count and I can spell, so I think I can help."

There are a lot of crates, and what could it hurt now, really? In for a penny, in for a pound, or whatever Lindy says. And as we search, I'm glad to have her here. Soon my jeans are smeared with filthy prints after wiping my dusty hands on my pants, and despite the cool in the basement, sweat beads up under my arms from climbing shelves and monkeying between the stacks. Jessa has a general idea where the oldest batches of patient folders are, and after what seems like hours but probably isn't, we've found the 1998 files between us. Anxious now, I stumble onto the *S*'s first. Wow, are there plenty. The first crate alone only goes up to Scollay. In the second I find the many Scotts and thumb through dozens of them with shaking hands, then do it again.

"Is it there?" Jessa asks, her chin nearly on my shoulder, her familiar cinnamon-gum breath in my face.

"Hold on." I grimace and flip through the folders more slowly this time. Scott, Rebecca. Scott, Samantha. Scott, Shawn. . . . Scott, Spencer. Scott, Thomas. "It's not in here."

"What? Look again."

"I looked again." I start to riffle through a fourth time, but stop myself. It's not here. Panicking won't help. I shove the crate back and think.

"Maybe you have the wrong name?" Jessa pipes up.

"I'm not stupid—" I start to snap, then pause. Because Miles Faye, handsome forensic pathologist, would ask himself, What do you *know*?

So what do you *know*, Imogene?

I suppose I don't know for certain that my mother hasn't been to Good Shepherd in the past seven years for a broken arm or something, that Sidonie Scott's file isn't active and up there in the HIS department with poor, clueless, keyless Mrs. Masciarelli. But if it is, what can I do about it? Breaking into a dusty storage room in the basement is one thing; breaking into the records department of a busy hospital, another. So I set that worry aside for the moment.

I know my mother's name is Sidonie, more or less admitted by Dad and confirmed by the dedication. I know she gave birth in this hospital in 1998, confirmed by . . . well, my birth. That's about it. And even so . . .

"I don't know her maiden name," I say. "She might have used her maiden name, right? Your mom does. People do that."

Jessa frowns. "Haven't you seen your birth certificate or anything? Like when you got your license?"

"No. Dad came with me and handled all that."

"And you never *asked*?"

"Of course I *asked*. Dad's . . . sensitive about stuff like that." Asking to hear my bedtime story was one thing. He never minded telling me stories. But pestering Dad for details about Mom, especially in the bad times, was wise only if I wanted to watch him wallow for days in a pit of sadness and empty beer cans and late-night infomercials.

"Okay." She blows out a breath that stirs years of dust into the air. "So we look for Sidney Something? Like that won't take forever."

"Sid-o-nie," I correct. There can't be many of them, but the boxes for 1998 fill five shelves, and we definitely don't have forever. I hop off the stacks I'm straddling, zip open my bag in the corner, and extract *A Time to Chill*. I turn to the dedication page, as if the information I'm looking for will magically appear in the text. Surprise! It doesn't. I flip through the whole book quickly.

This is the best clue I have. It led me to Good Shepherd Hospital. It led me to the storage room in the basement. Maybe her last name is here somewhere. I turn it over in my hands, read the back cover.

"Find the *F*'s," I say. "All of them for 1998."

Jessa digs right in through the cobwebs, and I'm sort of shocked by her cooperation. I climb back up and between us we zero in on the first box of *F*'s. There are fewer than the *S*'s, thank god, and before long I land on a thin file that drains the blood from my head and pounds it right into my heart.

Faye, Sidonie.

SIX

"But we have to go to the Friendly Toast," Jessa says, examining herself in the mirror in the second-floor bathroom half an hour later.

"Just go without me. I'll take the train home."

"Ugh, by yourself? Last time I took it this guy sat down and clipped his fingernails right next to me. He got skin cells in my umbrella."

"I've done it lots of times before." I've always ridden with Dad, but I don't say so. I wouldn't mind taking the commuter rail, would love the chance to read my mother's file while the train winds toward Sugarbrook between so many lakes, you'd think Massachusetts was just a thin film of land over endless, bottomless water. It's a cold two-mile walk from the train and bus station to my house on Cedar Lane, but that might be better than calling Lindy for a ride.

"But I already told my brother you're coming. . . ." Jessa smiles, playing her best card. Chad Price hardly cares if I show, much to my perpetual disappointment, and the last thing I'm in the mood for is clumsy flirting over all-day breakfast burritos.

"I'm all dusty and spiderwebby. I look like the Crypt Keeper."

"You look, like, amazing," she says while studying her own reflection, which is pretty close to perfect in her awesome yellow jacket, black skinny cords, and tan Bebe heels with gold tips. After a few strokes of a pocket comb, her hair flows across her shoulders in an unrumpled sheet. One coat of Baby Lips pink-tinted lip balm, and it's easy to see why she's never needed her own car, or even a license. A girl like Jessa rides in boys' cars, and they think she's doing them a favor.

Because my outfit was meant to be functional for thievery *and* inspire sympathy in Dr. Van Tassel, the overall look is Mission: Pathetic. From black (but really gray) tennis shoes to old black jeans loose in all the wrong places to a shapeless black puffy coat Dad bought me last year (Lindy, mouth twisted in sympathy,

offered to return it and buy me something more fashionable, after which I wanted nothing more than to keep
it), I'm not dressed for success. I am wearing one of my
favorite shirts, at least, a long-sleeve tee with the entire
text of Dad's latest book, *A Shriek in the Dark*, printed
on it in very, very small type. He bought this one at a
mystery writers' conference in New Jersey, and I wore
it to school the next day: senior picture day, to Lindy's
dismay. Lindy would prefer I wear blouses instead of
T-shirts. I genuinely wish I knew what separates a blouse
from a T-shirt. Fancier fabric? Ruffles?

And though I swear my mousy hair was in a neat
ponytail this morning—the better not to be mistaken for
a rogue mental patient in the halls of Good Shepherd—
hours of climbing the stacks in a dirty basement have
mussed it every which way. Jessa does what she can with
tap water to smooth it back and offers me her mini can
of hairspray wordlessly.

I frown into the mirror. "This is useless. Just leave
me."

"Never. Come on, Jeremy will be there. It's
important."

"Finding my dad is important. Eating hash browns
while you sit on Jeremy White's lap? I'm thinking less so.
I just want to go home and be alone and read the file."

"With Lindy kicking down your bedroom door?

Come eat. Have fun, you know? Experience, like, joy? And Chad will drive us home and you can spend the night reading in peace. I'll help you. Or okay, I won't bug you. Whatevs."

I accept the mini hairspray.

"Fab!" She beams. "Just one more thing . . ." Jessa digs Mrs. Masciarelli's keys out of her coat pocket, pulls open one of the stall doors, and hangs the key ring on the purse hook mounted inside. "HIS is just down the hall. She'll find them on her next bathroom run."

I admit, Jessa has a mind for detective work. She knows how to get what she wants, and get away clean. As far as accomplices go, I could do worse than Jessa Price.

To meet Chad and Jeremy we walk down to Boston Common, a little ways from Good Shepherd, toward the Park Street station. Road salt, foot traffic, and a few warm days have whipped the sidewalk snow into gray foam. It isn't warm tonight, not even for February, and it's dark outside already. But there are people everywhere. Mostly couples. A pale boy and girl in matching lavender skinny jeans hold hands on the platform at Park. On the red line to Kendall Square, a curvy girl in a pink Sox sweatshirt sits on her boyfriend's lap, her hair a slick purple-black curtain around their faces, and though the seat next to them is perfectly good, no one wants to sit in it, thank you very much.

Jessa's watching them, her face a mask of vague horror. All I really care about is the file weighing down my bag, but if there's anything you should read only in a special place and not in a T car smelling of Chinese food and wet clothing, it's this. To stop myself from pulling it out, I read a poster warning riders to report "mysterious packages" four times before departing the train in Cambridge.

The Friendly Toast is a short, cold walk from the Kendall stop. It's one of Dad's favorite places in Boston. We used to go after sessions, and now we stop by after a movie or music on the Common. The walls are lime green, decorated with old movie posters and cuckoo clocks, tin signs for funny-sounding beers, and life-size ratty-haired Barbies. I'm not dumb or desperate enough to think I'll find Dad with a drink at the bright pink bar, but I can't help looking while we stomp the slush off our shoes. No dice.

Across the restaurant, Chad and Jeremy wave at us from one of the big laminated tables under a giant, mustachioed plastic cheeseburger wearing a sombrero.

We spent so long in the stacks that we're late in arriving and the boys have their huge plates of greasy breakfast food already. Jessa tucks herself into a chair beside Jeremy White. I hug my bag and perch restlessly on the seat next to Chad, who smiles at me, his mouth tiled with impossibly square white teeth, his lightly freckled nose scrunching. "What's up, Imogene?" he says in his deep voice, gravel-low.

A sophomore at BU, Chad Price is pure blond, white blond, with long, nearly white eyelashes and pale green eyes. You'd think he'd be a ghost with hair like that, but his face is winter tanned from ranging the Marple Slopes, where he works part-time as a ski instructor when he's not studying organic chemistry and preparing to take the MCATs next year. Once I asked Chad why he wanted to be a doctor. He shrugged and said he likes working with his hands, which are blond-furred and big-knuckled and generally divine. We've played countless games of Super Smash Bros. on the WiiU in the Prices' basement, and sometimes when he knocks my Kirby off into space, he cackles gloatingly, reaches over, and shakes me by the back of the neck. After which I'm so flushed, I'm easily punted out of bounds the moment I'm reborn. Does this make me pathetic? Très. It gets worse, because then I walk home and spend the night cultivating a case of longing so vigorous, I'm almost proud of it.

So I have a crush. A crush is not a contract. I am obligated to do nothing more than feel all my feelings and then close them up and put them back on the shelf, to be taken out and revisited like any familiar story that feels safe precisely because the ending never changes.

"Im doesn't want to talk to you, *Chadwick*," Jessa scolds. "She's, like, preoccupied."

He lifts an eyebrow paler than his skin. "On a Saturday night?"

"And she's sleeping over, so don't bother us."

"Sleepover?" Jeremy snakes an arm around Jessa's waist. "But I didn't bring my toothbrush."

Chad reaches over to smack Jeremy, who karate-blocks Chad to protect his 'do: a stiff black faux-hawk like the bone ridge on a dinosaur's skull.

They're Best Friends for Life, or whatever the boy equivalent is. I've never understood it. Chad records every episode of *How It's Made* and will describe the creation of a crayon in the same reverent tone you'd use to talk about the miracle of flight; Jeremy watches You-Tube compilations of the world's worst car crashes. But buddies they are, and if Chad objects to Jeremy dating his sister, it's never stopped them. Not since Jessa was a bright, shiny sophomore and Jeremy the senior soccer captain. Jessa can never decide if she loves or hates Jeremy. At this nanosecond in time they're broken up, have been since Jeremy went on a two-week Caribbean Christmas cruise with his family and didn't bother telling

Jessa, and only brought her back a puka-shell bracelet from the airport newsstand. Jessa and Jeremy fight easily and often. But by the moony look in her eyes as she plucks a potato wedge from his plate, I'm fairly certain she's cycling around to love. They'll be back together by June, just in time for the holy of holies (Sugarbrook High's prom, which I'm pretty set on *not* attending).

What do I know about it, anyway? A two-month relationship with Lee Jung was my longest to date. He made me three retro-romantic mix CDs of love songs last Valentine's Day, and I hyperventilated in my car for half an hour, then ended things with a text. The only other Valentine I got was from Dad—he bought me SweeTarts, his favorite candy, and I bought him a Kalev bitter dark chocolate bar, my favorite, only so we could make a show of hiding them from each other. To see who could find and steal the other's bounty first, you know? Dad won, excavating his SweeTarts from my glove box. While it was locked. While my also-locked Civic sat in the Sugarbrook High student lot. Dad's a writer; he's researched lots of stuff, including ways to break into anything, and afterward he taught me. This Valentine's Day . . . maybe a stone heart counts as a Valentine after all.

Busy fiddling with the straps on my satchel, I don't realize Jessa's talking to me until she leans across the table and sticks a wedge in my face. "Hello? I said relax. We'll work on that *project* tonight, okay?"

I grab it and take a small, reluctant bite.

"What project?" Chad asks.

"Math, nosy. We're trying to figure out how many morons it takes to order two smoking-hot teenage girls some dinner." She smiles into Jeremy's ear.

"Not hungry," I say.

Chad slides his plate over to me, still half-filled with his massive omelet. "Want to share? I can't even finish it. I'll roll down the slopes tomorrow." He leans back and pats his stomach, which makes a sound like slapping the hard, tight skin of a drum.

I smooth back my ponytail anxiously. If Jessa knows my dad's MIA, I wonder if Chad knows. Searching his clear green eyes just long enough to look for pity, I find none. Good. I would hate for him to find out.

I dig into the remains of the omelet so he won't suspect anything's wrong. He grins and I am momentarily dazzled, which feels 50 percent like fire in my chest and 50 percent like cold panic. I look away and shove a big, cheesy bite in my mouth. I don't have the time or the heart to be dazzled.

It's late when we pull into the Prices' circular driveway. Chad parks his Jeep in their three-car garage, packed to the rafters with grown-up toys like mountain bikes and ski poles and kayaks and golf clubs. Jessa's family is big on expensive outdoor sports; they've even got a medium-size boat docked in Buzzards Bay to the east, which is why big, shiny fishing poles hang on a rack by Dr. Van Tassel's convertible.

Our (considerably smaller) garage is stacked with Tupperware bins of my baby clothes and stuffed animals, blurry photos of a youthful Ma Ma and Grandpa Scott, Halloween decorations we haven't untangled in a decade. Old and mostly useless things Dad never looks at but couldn't bring himself to get rid of when Lindy moved in and we needed the space, so now it's out there, exiled but preserved. No pictures or sweaters or fishing poles from Sidonie Faye, though. Believe me, I've checked.

"You sure you don't want to stop by your place and grab your stuff real quick?" Jessa asks once Chad's out of the car.

"Very sure." There is no chance of a "real quick" stop. I left a voice mail on Lindy's cell a little while ago, when I knew her precise bedtime schedule had placed her in the shower. Easier to stay away and stay mad about our ill-fated road trip if I don't have to hear my stepmother's voice.

We let ourselves in through the garage door that

leads into the big metallic kitchen. The lights are off; Dr. Van Tassel's shift won't end till eleven and Mr. Price is in bed already, still adjusting to US time after his business trip. Jessa stops to grab us Cokes out of the fridge while I wave off Chad, who heads down to his basement. We make our way to Jessa's room on the second floor, every part of it familiar. Her pastel peach walls are plastered with photos of the Prices' vacations—the whole shimmering blond family glowing and sunburned on a cruise to the Bahamas; kid-Jessa and Chad sword-fighting with baguettes in front of the Eiffel Tower; her parents canoodling in a gondola in the narrow green waterways of Rome. Jessa reserves her vanity mirror for pictures of her and Jeremy. Her shelves are stocked with souvenir snow globes and tiny dolls and little statues Mr. Price brings home from trips. Her shirts and dresses and skinny pants have overflowed the closet and crept into the corners of her room, draped over an armchair patterned in bright red lips, flung into her satin laundry hamper, balled up on the white writing desk.

I could describe it as easily as my own bedroom after all these countless nights when we were supposedly hanging out, though mostly we were coexisting: Jessa doodling in notebooks or lip-synching to Taylor Swift, and me reading or daydreaming about how Chad's and my future wedding table numbers would be printed on

THE MYSTERY OF HOLLOW PLACES

pages copied from old medical textbooks. It was a solemn and sacred pastime, always.

While Jessa unzips her coat and boots, I dig through her pajama drawer. Pushing aside the Victoria's Secret stuff—why would anyone want so many pairs of sweatpants with PINK stamped on the butt? That's the real secret—I settle on a pair of striped drawstring pants and a tank top with cupcakes hugging on the chest.

"So," Jessa says, and claps. "Let's do this."

"Can I—can I wash up first?" I ask.

She shrugs. "You know where everything is."

I pad down the hall and into Jessa's bathroom, where I grab a new toothbrush out of a basket under the sink and wash my face with her twilight-roses cleanser, then take my time dabbing on her midnight-violets toner. I brush out my ponytail and loop my hair into a loose bedtime braid, patiently smoothing out the bumps. When I've run out of grooming tools I know how to use—though lilac under-eye butter and cashmere-infused hair lotion sound intriguing—I lean over and grip the sides of the sink, the porcelain slick and cool on my shaky, sweaty palms.

It's funny—all night I've wanted nothing more than to dig into my mom's file, and now that it's time . . . I want to be ready, but I feel like . . . I feel exactly like handsome forensic pathologist Miles Faye in *A Bitter*

Taste, the fourth book in Dad's series. Miles is investigating the death of a grade school buddy, a guy he hasn't seen in ages. Just before he opens the postmortem report, where he'll find massive amounts of illegal drugs in the blood panel, he sees this clear picture of him and his friend lying around in the scruff of the overgrown ball field by their childhood homes. He sees the bare blue sky and the sun streaming pink through his closed eyelids, and he feels the warm dust under him thirty years later, and his own breathlessness from the race they've just run across the field. Idyllic, right? As Miles picks up the report, he knows that what he's holding has the power to tarnish that snapshot, so he'll never again call it to mind and remember being so young and warm without feeling the cold breath of time on them both.

Not that I think my mom's file will tell me she's a drug addict or anything. Besides, it's seventeen years old, so the info won't exactly be current. It's just that I've been imagining her for so long, and this is the end of imagining and the start of knowing. It's kind of terrifying.

But I stare into my own brown eyes in the bathroom mirror and grit out, "Don't be an asshole. You're doing this for Dad."

I make myself march to the bedroom, where I sit cross-legged on Jessa's floral bedspread and pull the manila folder out of my bag. Avoiding Jessa's eyes as she eases onto the bed beside me, I touch the stone heart in my front pocket.

I open the folder.

Inside are maybe a dozen slightly yellowed papers, crisp with age. The first is a maternity preregistration form, stamped with the shepherd's crook logo of Good Shepherd Hospital. It's dizzying how much is here. I read through the *patient information* section greedily.

Patient's name exactly as it appears on ID: Faye, Sidonie Gene

Date of birth: 1/22/1977

Pausing to do the math, I realize my mother is fourteen years younger than my father, who'll be fifty-two this year. When I was born, she was only four years older than I am.

Expected date of delivery: 4/9/1998

Race: Caucasian

Marital status: Single

I stop, reread. That can't be right. When her file showed up under "Faye," I figured Mom had pulled a Dr. Van Tassel and kept her name. My parents were married. Dad told me so, and he told Lindy . . . except even as I think it, I wonder if Lindy's ever seen the divorce papers. It's possible he lied to both of us. I can feel myself start to sink, because if Dad lied about this, then everything I thought I knew becomes a little less certain, and the few facts I've accumulated in my life aren't stone, but sand.

But I can't start doubting my dad. He always told me the truth, even the few times when I wished he wouldn't. So this must mean something. It's what Miles Faye would call an "inconsistency in the story," and inconsistencies are valuable. They're the smoke that warns of fire. It tells me there has to be something here.

"Find anything?" Jessa asks.

I shake my head, keep reading.

Patient's home address: 42 Cedar Lane, Sugarbrook, MA 01703

Patient's current employer: Boston Museum of Fine Arts

Patient's occupation: Assistant to the curator of prints and drawings

To think, all the school trips we've taken to the MFA over the years. What if Sidonie Faye was somewhere in those halls, in one of the offices, grabbing an overpriced lunch in the cafeteria? Finding her can't be as easy as a trip to the museum, and it has been seventeen years. She can't still be there. But it might be worth a visit.

I skip past her social security number—I know it would be useful if I was *actually* a detective, but alas— down a few unhelpful lines to *Emergency contact.* I expect it will be my dad, but it isn't.

Emergency contact: Lillian Ward
Home number: 978-555-8761
Relationship: Cousin

That's something I can use. Everything else on the form is under *Insurance information* and some category called a *Guarantor*. That last one is my dad, and none of it is new info.

Next in the folder are a lot of notes from her admittance to Good Shepherd. How many weeks pregnant, date of last menstruation, para and gravida births (zero and zero, whatever that means), vital signs, dilation and effacing (ugh). Contractions, CBC results. I skip through most of it, until—

Is the patient on any prescribed medication? Nortriptyline (Pamelor)

"Hey, can I look something up on your—"

"What do you need?" Jessa asks, browser up on her phone, thumbs at the ready.

"Um. Can you find out what Pamelor's for? It's a—"

"A second-generation tri . . . tri-cyc-lic? Antidepressant used in the treatment of major depression, and for childhood nocturnal ensu . . . ensur-esis? Whatever, bed-wetting."

I grind my bottom lip between my teeth. "I'm guessing she wasn't a bed wetter." Flipping ahead through the pages, most everything else is about my birth. Something called an Apgar score. A copy of my tiny, inky footprints. PKU results. When and how I breastfed, baby's first pee and poo. Yikes, it's thorough. There's a note at the very bottom of the last page that catches my eye:

Patient is bonding with infant.

I put the papers away and close the folder gently, then pull my legs up and hug my knees, breathing in and out.

"Sooo . . ." Jessa clears her throat. "Are you okay?"

Nodding, I breathe in and out and in. Maybe I shouldn't be okay. The information *is* somewhat ominous. But honestly, it explains a lot. It's like I've been driving through fog and rain and now the weather is starting to clear, the road just ahead of me sharpening, coming into focus. Before tonight, I had only my dad's word to go on, my bedtime story, and of course I trust him. But here's real evidence that my mother was sick. That she needed saving. And whether or not Lindy wants to believe, I'm starting to get why my dad is searching for her.

"This is good," I say, to myself and to Jessa. "This helps."

"Awesome! So where do we start?"

"No offense, but I think I want to just do it by

myself. You know? But . . . thanks," I finish lamely.

She snorts. "Okay. Except maybe you should've figured that out before you, like, dragged me to the hospital."

"I didn't—" I start to protest.

"Oh, whatever!" She jumps off the bed and plops dramatically down on a nest of leggings in her lips chair, arms slicing the air. "You think I'm an idiot, right? Jeez, sorry *I* didn't get 2230 on *my* SATs. But you're not as smart as you think, because I know you lied about your dad—you're lying to the police, and Lindy, and I know you lied to my mom. You lied to me about shopping. And you lied about your car being in the shop all weekend, 'cause I saw it at your house just now when we drove by, oh most brilliant genius. Don't deny it—I'm a way better liar than you. You could've gone to the hospital by yourself. You decided you needed me, but, what, you don't trust me?"

The rough edges of the stone saw into my fingertips. "So what if I lied? I'm the one that has to find him."

"By you, you mean the cops, yes?"

"Yeah, right. They don't know my dad."

Jessa's bright blue eyes are so wide, they're almost floating. "I'm not trying to be a bitch, Im, but he never told you anything about your mom, and he didn't tell you he was peacing out, and he hasn't told you where he is. So maybe you don't know him either."

"He did tell me!" I say, shoving the file into my bag and tumbling the heart in after it. "He's looking for my mother. My real mom, I mean. I think he's trying to help her."

"But why now, after this long?"

"I haven't figured that out. But if I can find her, I'll find him."

I never should've come to the Prices'. I stand to leave, to walk home and slip in the back and sneak to my bedroom, where I can lock myself in alone, like I wanted from the start.

"Okay, okay, okay, wait." Jessa vaults up and into my path. I start to slink around her and she blocks me. I fake right, but she spreads her arms and beats me to the left. "If you really think that's where your dad is, I can help. And I *am* a better liar than you."

I hover between the bed and the door. "Why do you even want to help?"

"Isn't that what best friends do?"

I pause, because honestly I don't know. It seems true. I sigh and drop the bag, if not my doubts. "I guess."

"Great! And anyway"—she shrugs and twirls a strand of hair—"it's February break. There's nothing else to do. Except Mackenzie Winn's party."

"Wait, what party?"

"At Mackenzie's. Next Saturday?"

"No one told me about a party," I say, a little hurt. I'm in mock trial with Mackenzie.

Jessa purses her lips, has the grace to look guilty. "I was going to."

SEVEN

I wake the next morning with a shirtless vampire eye-sexing me. Puzzling, when I'm still dragging myself out of my dream by my fingertips. In the dream, I was driving down a road striped with power lines and stippled with leaf-light through the trees. It was peaceful until I came raging through, swerving and clipping the guardrail like I was drunk, that dizzy feeling I remember from the night Lee Jung and I hijacked his parents' Goldschläger. But in the dream I was clear-headed, just unable to control the car, or my foot like a fifty-pound weight on the gas, or the spasming steering wheel. I knew there was somewhere I need to be, something I needed to get to, and might, if only I could drive in a straight line.

Maybe my dreams are trying to tell me something.

It's a short, muddled moment before the whys and the wheres coming floating back out of the fog. I'm in Jessa's bed, smashed against the big *Vampire Diaries* poster tacked to her bedroom wall. I'm here and not in my own bed because Dad is missing, has been missing for four days. As I realize this an ache settles in my chest; not a weight, but an absence. A pocket of nothingness inside me.

Then I roll over and see Jessa drooling on her floral pillowcase, uncharacteristically rumpled. Weirdly I feel shy, remembering the night before, my tantrum, and afterward in the quiet bedroom, the sounds of her breathing so close to me when we'd turned the lights out. It was nice, having a friend there in the dark while I pieced together an imperfect picture of my mother.

My mother bonded with me at birth.

My mother was once an assistant to the curator of prints and drawings at the Boston Museum of Fine Arts.

My mother wasn't even twenty-one when she gave birth to me.

My mother was taking pills for major depression.

My mother has a cousin.

I remember our project for the day and sit up with a

start. I catapult off the mattress, careful not to catch a foot on my friend.

She curls into the sheets. "Ugh," she groans. "What are you *doing?*"

"We have an emergency contact to find."

"It's Sunday. It's seven o'clock. On a *Sunday.*"

"I can't sleep anymore."

"You could if you tried. I even gave you the Damon Salvatore side of the bed. What a waste." She jabs her finger at the fanged blond on the poster. Rolling, she reaches out and caresses his pale paper face. "Good morning, lover."

"What does Jeremy think of the Damon Salvatore side of the bed?"

She sits up and half smiles, arches her back, catlike. "He wouldn't give a shit if it was a Yankees poster. I have a bed and a door that locks."

"What a prince." I squat and dig through her pants drawer, hoping for something, anything, in a size bigger than two. Taking Jessa's help? It's . . . difficult. Taking her pants? Not a problem.

"Oh, whatever. I'm, like, seventeen."

I choose not to ponder the fact that although I'm also seventeen, the "highlight" of my sex life has been a few heavy-breathing-and-pants-rubbing sessions in Lee Jung's TV room, while *Reservoir Dogs* played and shouted and bled on the big screen and my head fizzed with the Goldschläger.

Jessa watches me root through her pants. "I take it you're not going home."

I stiffen. "I can go home. If you're busy or something—"

"You know that's not what I'm saying. Here." She takes mercy on me and tosses me a pair of black leggings with zippered ankles draped across the headboard.

I lift them tentatively.

"They're totally clean! And slimming!"

"Oh gosh, thanks."

"With this, with this!" Jessa leaps up and plunges into her vaulted closet, emerging with a slouchy red sweaterdress, a big black heart glittering across the back. "And this!" She thrusts a necklace at me, a long black chain with little gold charms and red beads and doodly-bobs jingling on the end. I have to admit it's a cool ensemble, but this seems like a strange day for dress-up. Maybe sensing this, she shrugs. "If you think you look good, you'll be more confident and stuff."

Who am I to argue? It works for Jessa.

I take my bounty and my purse and leave Jessa alone with Damon Salvatore. Darting down the hall so I won't be caught by Chad with happy cupcakes on my breasts, I shut myself in the bathroom. Strange day for dress-up though it may be, I pull and clasp and stuff myself into Jessa's outfit like it's armor. I brush my hair into a careful sleek ponytail, swipe on some not particularly daring brown eyeliner I found rolling around my purse bottom, and stare myself down in the mirror. Embarrassed by last night's cowardice, I tell myself that for the next twenty-four hours I am an unstoppably brilliant badass detective. I'm Emily Pollifax, Lisbeth Salander, Annika Bengtzon.

I'm Miles fucking Faye.

When I get back to the bedroom, Jessa's still under the covers, but zipping a finger across her iPad screen like the professional she is. Neither of us could find a Sidonie Faye online, because of course it wouldn't be so easy so soon. But hers isn't the only name I've got. Officer Griffin and the police will be talking to Dad's limited family—a fistful of cousins scattered across the West Coast, an uncle in Chicago, Grandpa Scott in a nursing home for Alzheimer's patients, for what that's worth.

But I have my mother's family.

"Okay, so there're a few Lillian Wards on Facebook," Jessa says. "But I don't think they're the right ages."

"Huh. What's that 978 area code?"

Tap, tap, swipe. "Shrewsbury. That's like half an hour southwest, right?" Swipe, tap, tap, type. While she works she chews the inside of her lip, a familiar and (almost) unattractive tic that only escapes when she's concentrating too hard to worry about looking unattractive. "Okay, nothing about her in the White Pages. But here's something else for Lillian Eugene, maiden name Lillian Ward." She tilts the screen toward me.

"What's 'Intellux'?"

"It's one of those professional background-check sites Mrs. Ginsberg told us about in Global Communications class. Companies can pay to look up the dirt on employees before hiring them—property records, criminal history, social media search. This is just the stuff we can see without paying."

"Wow. Can you try Sidonie Faye?"

It's a long shot; if her name were on this site, it would've turned up in a search. As expected, nothing. "Maybe it just means no companies have done a background check on her in a while."

I sit on the bed beside her and gobble up what crumbs of info there are. Relatives: Michael Ward, Elizabeth Ward. Married Name: Lillian Eugene. Address history: Fitchburg, MA; Shrewsbury, MA; Worcester, MA.

Worcester is just one town farther than Shrewsbury.

"Look for Lillian Eugene on Facebook, and see if there are any of them in Worcester."

"One sec . . . okay, ta-da! Here's one in Worcester.

And jeez . . ." She frowns. "She only has thirteen friends. Poor lady."

I take the iPad. Lillian Eugene's account looks like the kind a grown-up sets up for the sole purpose of playing Candy Crush. There are regular status updates, totally factual statements like "What a hot day it is today." "Went to see a movie last night and liked it very much." And the latest: "Spring-cleaning my classroom. Work on a Sunday morning is not much fun." She has thirteen friends indeed, and almost no comments. Talk about shouting into the void. None of these friends are Sidonie Anything, or Anybody Faye. I open her photos page to find exactly one picture, her profile, a close-up of her face. Middle-aged, with very short, wispy hair more ashen than blond, and webs of wrinkles in the corners of her colorless gray eyes.

"Is it her?" Jessa plunks a finger down on Lillian Eugene's face.

"I can't tell." I hold the screen closer, searching for a trace of me in her. It's a hard sell. I look a lot like my dad, who inherited his facial features and dark, straight hair from my Chinese grandmother, then passed a weaker strain on to me. We have the same brown eyes and thin noses and natural frowns. But maybe there's something in Lillian's round cheeks and narrow chin, a heart-shaped face, like Mom's in her picture in *A Time to Chill.* Like mine. Dad doesn't have one, for sure. "It could be. I mean, it might."

"What is she, your aunt?"

"Second cousin."

"Okay, so send her a message."

I float my finger over the screen, hesitating. It just doesn't seem right. In Nancy Drew's day she had to worry whether suspicious Taylor Sinclair would spot the beam of her flashlight as she followed him through the mysterious Mayan exhibit at the museum. Now I have to worry whether to tip off my second cousin that I'm Facebook-stalking her. "I don't know."

"Think about it. My morning breath is distracting me."

While Jessa goes and washes up in the bathroom and does what she does to pop out looking like America's Next Top Model, I sit cocooned in her flowered quilt, trying to make her iPad do my bidding. I might be the only kid in the school district who doesn't know how to use one. A few birthdays ago I complained to Dad, but he just patted me on the head and said, "Suffering helps the soul to grow."

Flicking clumsily through Lillian's profile, I bring up her contact info. There's no phone number. But in the employment section, it lists St. Augustine High in Worcester. I check her status update about spring cleaning and see that it was posted less than an hour ago.

As I'm banging on the bathroom door, Jessa emerges, face dripping and hair piled atop her head with a big claw clip. "Jesus, what?"

"How fast can you be ready to go?"

"Umm . . ." She looks in the mirror, does some mental math. "Half hour?"

"Can you do, like, ten minutes?"

She twists her lips. "I can do seventeen."

"Sold."

Jessa keeps her word, and an hour later we're navigating the uncharming streets of Worcester, Massachusetts, in my Civic, which we rescued from my driveway in a stealth operation. By which I mean we ran through the wind to my house, hopped in, shut the car doors softly, and peeled out of there before Lindy could peek through the curtains.

I'll have to face her sometime today, but who knows how long it will take Lillian Eugene to clean out her classroom?

"Turn right here, at the gas station." Jessa points toward a street just past a Sunoco. She sort of knows Worcester; she was carted down by her family a few times a year for Chad's high school soccer matches against Burncoat High and Claremont Academy. But she's never seen St. Augustine, a stone megalith that looms over the corner of Elm. Round towers like castle turrets, narrow slots for windows, a big marble statue of a robed saint feeding a deer in the courtyard.

"Oh good." Jessa frowns as I park in the lot around back. "We're breaking into Jesus school."

"We're not breaking in," I say, surveying the lot. There's a little green car across the way, speckled gray with mud and dust. "We're . . . scoping out."

"Is that hers, you think?" Jessa nods her chin at the car.

"It's the only car here."

"What if she went home?"

"Then we'll ask whoever it is about her. Obviously they work here."

"So . . . we scope?"

"We scope."

The wind whips our hair as we step outside into the weather, growing steadily darker and more miserable. The clouds are a solid gray block above us, low hanging, and the ice in the air burns my nostrils on the inhale. Wednesday's warm snap has definitely passed. I duck down inside my puffy coat, wishing I hadn't put on such thin armor; wishing I had a tissue; wishing, most of all, that I could be the kind of detective unfazed by problems so petty as cold legs and a runny nose.

We book it to the grimy car across the lot. Jessa tucks her fingers into her jacket sleeve and reaches to wipe the frost off the passenger side window.

"Wait," I say. "There might be an alarm."

"Please, it's a Saturn SL." She clears the glass. "I see a cat bobblehead on the dashboard," she says through chattering teeth. "Does that help?"

"Yes, immensely." I peek in through the driver side window. Empty except for a coffee thermos in the cup holder and a few Petco bags full of cleaning supplies on the gray cloth seats. I don't know what I expected to find.

Jessa tugs on the driver side door handle.

"Whoa, felon."

"Oh, it's locked anyway. So now what?"

"We wait for someone to come out, I guess?"

We retreat to the Civic and I turn the key so heat leaks out of the vents. While we wait I sneak a look at Jessa, gorgeously flushed in the cold. Her abbreviated prep time hasn't done her any harm. What would I do with all that beauty if it were mine? What would I worry about if I had perfect skin and expertly shaped nails and a miniature nose and a perfect house and a brilliant mother and a normal father whose only shortcoming was sinking a little too deeply into his boring work stories at the dinner table?

I know Jessa must have her own problems, the most often spoken of being true love. She loves Jeremy, then she loves Levi Cantu, then she loves Mike Wazchowitz, then she's letting Jeremy unhook her bra in his dorm room at BU and loving him more than anything. Maybe that's what comes of having the perfect life. You've got nothing to do with your time but love everybody just *that* much.

When I think of it that way, it sounds like a problem I don't ever want.

An hour later the side exit of St. Augustine swings open and a squat woman wobbles out onto the grassy moat around the school, then into the parking lot, her head so far down in the wind that she's practically tipped forward.

"Hey, hey!" Jessa, preoccupied with Fruit Ninja after growing bored by our stakeout, has looked up from her phone and elbows me unnecessarily.

"Yeah, I see her." I shoulder open my door and without a moment's hesitation call out, "Hi, excuse me, are you Lillian Eugene, by any chance?"

The woman slows, than continues forward. Close up, I can see she's a small woman, the pom-pom perched on her winter hat no higher than my chin, swaddled in a bulky winter jacket that gives her the figure of the Michelin Man. A scarf is wrapped around the lower half of her face, but her eyes peek out, gray like sky overcast by filmy clouds. They wince suspiciously. "Are you a student?" she mumbles through her scarf. "No students allowed in the lot on Sundays."

"I'm, um . . ." I feel the panic swell up inside me, until I remember that I'm Miles Faye, and I'm bullet-proof. "Do you know a Sidonie Faye?"

The scarf drops, revealing the hard line of her puckered lips. She swipes a stray hair out of her face gracelessly. "Do you?"

I swallow. "I wish."

EIGHT

Two blocks from St. Augustine, my second cousin lives in a faded brick apartment building gridded with rust-stained balconies. On the inside it's clean enough, though there are no elevators, the hallways are cold and dim, and a damp locker-room smell seeps up from the tangerine carpet. Lillian Eugene leads the way up five flights of stairs to apartment 54B. Settling her bag on one hip, she jiggles her key in the lock, opens the door a sliver, and sticks a boot inside before threading the rest of her body through. "Come quick, before the babies escape."

Jessa and I slip into the front hallway, where we're pinned by the yellow moon eyes of five gigantic gray cats.

"Did my babies miss me? Did they miss me very much?" Lillian coos as the cats rub their faces on her snow boots and melt between her legs. "Was Mama gone forever and ever? Did you miss Mama? You did?" Somehow she makes it to the closet without trampling a tail or a paw.

I've forgotten Jessa until she leans in and whispers, "What's that word that means a vision?"

"What?" I whisper back.

"Like, say I just had a vision of tomorrow's front page headline, 'Teenage Girls Fed Poisoned Butterscotches in Worcester Apartment, Beautiful Faces Eaten by Cats.' What would you call that?"

"A premonition. And stop." I shrug her off. "Thanks for having me up here . . . Ms. Eugene."

"Call me Lil. But I can't talk too long—just popping in to feed the babies, and then I'm running out." She strips out of her heavy winter coat. Underneath, she's a sharp, thin woman nearly as colorless as her pets. Her short gray hair is a static halo around her face. She rolls up the sleeves of her shapeless gray sweater and studies me, and it strikes me that Lillian Eugene is not delighted by my presence. "You look like your father," she says matter-of-factly. Her eyes flick down to my chin, like my mother's, like Lil's. She smiles in a strained kind of way.

"Yes, I think so too."

We sit at the little plastic-topped kitchen table while she prepares the cats' food. To our left is a window that looks out into a multistory parking garage, and on the sill, a little ceramic planter that must've held something green and alive once, but now it's an empty socket, the soil inside filmed with dust. I squint in the headlights of a car as it parks directly across from us, its front bumper maybe ten feet from our chairs. "So this is a cute place," Jessa manages.

I shiver, noticing just now how cold it is in Lil's apartment.

"We get by here. Close to school, and enough room for me and my babies." She sets five bowls down on the floor and the cats cease their whining, attacking their food as one. Satisfied, Lil backs up against the counter. Jessa and I occupy the only two chairs in the kitchen, one of which Lil dragged in from another room. "So how'd you look me up?" she asks.

"Some old paperwork. Stuff my dad left lying around."

"He knows you're here?"

"No one knows." I keep it vague. I don't yet have

a reason to lie to my long-lost relative, but you never know when a reason will present itself. "You two haven't talked in a while?"

"What, me and your dad? Jesus, no." Lil plucks a piece of gray hair off her sweater—hers or her babies', I can't tell. "Not in forever. We fell out of touch. I fell out of touch with a lot of people after my divorce. That's the way it happens."

I don't know what to say to this. Should you apologize for hearing someone's ancient bad news, when by now they must be sick to death after years of hearing "I'm sorry"? "I guess Dad doesn't really keep in touch with most of Mom's family."

"No, he hasn't had much contact with us since your mama. Not that there're many of us left."

I can't help but deflate a little. I'd hoped Dad and I were sniffing along the exact same trail. But that doesn't mean there isn't a trail here. No one else can tell me what this woman can; no one else can tell me about *her*. Except my dad, and where is he? I fiddle with the charms on my borrowed necklace, fold my hands in my lap, crack my knuckles. "Who is left, then?"

"Not Sid's parents. My parents moved down south for the heat, and they won't be coming back. Can't say I blame them." Lil stoops and with a huff of pain, clumsily lowers her narrow body to the floor to sit among her cats, who drip over her like honey.

"Um, do you want my chair?" Jessa asks, red-faced, stroking her fingers through her hair furiously. "I can wait somewhere else."

"Oh, no." Lil shakes her head, smiling down on her pets. "I like it fine right here. What's good enough for my babies is good enough for me."

Jessa returns to staring nervously out the window into the parking garage, bouncing her leg under the table and chewing the inside of her lip.

"Is there any more of Mom's family around here?" I ask, trying to steer us straight. "I'd love to meet them. Dad never really talks about you all. Or, you know, my mom. Do you? Ever talk to her?"

"Sid? Lord, no. Not in years and years."

"How many? Would you say?"

"I guess five or six. The last time we talked I was still with Robert, but near the end. I remember, because he came down to my reading room in the old place, which he never came into, and said, 'It's one of your cousins on the phone for you,' and I said, 'I only have the one,' and he said, 'Yes, but didn't she run off?'"

"What did she say to you?"

"She wasn't saying too much. Sid and me were close once. When we were little in Fitchburg—I lived near the part I guess they don't call Tar Hill anymore, but they used to. Her mama was my daddy's sister. We were only kids, no other cousins around. I think there were more of our people out west, more Wards, but we never met them. I don't know about her daddy's side. Anyhow, her mom went off when Sid was young, and her daddy passed on when she was in high school, so Sid came and lived with us. Her daddy left a little insurance money for her, so when she graduated she took it and left to . . . what do you call it, study abroad? At a fancy art school in some country over there."

"Switzerland?" I ask, recalling my bedtime story.

"I think Sweden. Whichever, she left, and I never heard a peep from her. Don't think she meant to come back, till Siobhan died. That's your grandmother."

"How did she die?"

Lil looks up at me and her eyes narrow. "Exposure, I guess. Sleeping outside in the cold. Wouldn't your daddy know this?"

"I just—I thought I remembered him saying it was her heart."

She shrugs.

"So, she called you five years ago and said—"

"That she'd just left her job. She was a receptionist for some eye doctor's office. I don't know the name of it. Lion? Something like 'Lion.' Anyway, she wasn't there anymore and she needed some money. Wanted to know if me or Robert could wire it to a Western Union in Connecticut. I sent what I could."

"Where in Connecticut?"

"I don't remember that." Lil's eyes flicker to the clock ticking above the rusted stove. "I know what you're asking, and I don't know where she is . . ."

"Imogene."

"Right. I can't tell you where she is. Don't know who could. It's been too long, and the family isn't around anymore. Some moved away, most passed."

Defeated, I go to the next question on my list. "What was she like when you did know her?"

"She . . . was shy, when we were kids. Okay in school. She was good at art. Drawing. She loved those how-to-draw books. Animals, faces, fantasy stuff. She had one with her all the time. Sometimes we would camp out in one of our little backyards, you know. There wasn't any forest or anything behind our houses, just a yard. We'd sleep in this old army surplus tent of my father's, and Sid would spend the whole night drawing, oh, I don't know, trolls. Or unicorns. She always wanted to be an artist."

Another difference between us—I can barely draw a stick-gallows in hangman. "I guess that's why she went to art school."

"She never finished, though. Whatever she did at the museum, it wasn't something you needed a degree for, not back then. Now they say you need one to wash dishes."

Something sinuous wraps around my leg. I look down to discover one of the cats and resist the urge to kick it away. "Why didn't she finish school?"

"Sid met your daddy. Had you. And then . . ." Lil sighs deeply. "I talked to Sid the night she left you both, you know?"

Jessa is trying to catch my gaze, but I avoid her. She feels sorry for me. Well, she shouldn't. Because right now it isn't even me talking to Lil Eugene. It's Miles Faye, with one goal: to get to the bottom of this mystery and find my dad. I make that the stone truth and harden myself around it. "What did she— Did she tell you why?"

Her lips screw up into a tremulous line. "There was no good *why*. She was troubled waters. Like her mother. Siobhan was troubled waters too—that's what my own mama called her. Sid said your daddy would be better off, you would be better off, everyone would be better off. But I don't think anybody was ever better off for what that girl did."

The clock ticks away the silence while a cat with what might be a sinus condition jockeys for position in Lil's lap, wheezing and purring in turns. She stares into its snot-streaked face, and who knows what she sees there, but her voice is duller and distant when she speaks again.

"Well, I really got to be running out now."

Unexpectedly, Jessa leans across the table. "Im is your cousin and you just met her. Can't you stay for a while?"

Lil levers herself stiffly off the floor, shedding animals from her lap as she rises. "It's my doctor's appointment. Not supposed to be late. But I have some pictures and things, if you want to take them with you."

"That would be great. Anything you can give me. And maybe your number, so I can call you sometime? I'll leave mine in case you remember anything."

She hesitates in the kitchen doorway. "Just hold on a minute." With a last look, she ducks into the hallway.

I jump as Jessa slaps her hand over mine. "Okay, she's weird, Im. I mean, like, I know teachers are weird—I had Mrs. Marconi in sophomore year, and she had, like, a deli in her desk? Not chips or breath mints or anything. Lunch meat, pickles, huge bottles of Pepsi in the bottom drawer. But your second cousin is *unusual*."

"Maybe it's the curse," I say, fingering the stone in my pocket as I watch the biggest of the cats mount the kitchen counter, flop backward, and lick the dark fur between its legs.

"What curse?"

I shrug.

Lil makes her way back into the kitchen with a small stack of photos and time-rippled papers in her hands. "Here's all I got. That's my number on that sticky note, but it's a home phone. I don't see much need to carry a little phone around all the time. If I wanted to talk to anybody, I'd call. And I usually don't want to talk."

Greedily, I flip through the pictures. There's a fuzzy baby photo in the pile, a little bald, hazel-eyed girl wriggling on a patchwork quilt, her oversize head tilted toward the camera with great effort. In Dad's office there's a picture of me just like this. I'm maybe a few months old, wallowing on a blue shag rug strewn with soft, plasticized baby books, my enormous skull wobbling so precariously that even though it's a moment frozen on film, you could swear I'm about to face plant into *Goodnight Moon*. Dad insists "book" was my first word, though sometimes Lindy swears the first words out of my mouth must have been "I'm fine, I don't need any help, go away."

Next is a picture of two little girls, the younger in brown pigtails, the older one a dirty shade of blond. Mom and Lil stand on the lawn of a church. Lil surprises me by tapping the picture with a fingernail bitten down to the skin. "That's the church we used to walk to each week. And our mamas would let me and Sid take the long way around Crocker Field on the way to Sid's house for Sunday lunch. I swear you could hear the crack of the baseball bats from her backyard. Smell the hot dogs."

I nod, wondering what goes on in Sunday school—Dad and I are not church people, though I've been in one, for Ma Ma Scott's funeral.

In the next picture, Mom is still small, but alone by a wiry, forked birch tree in a front yard, the sky behind the little house awash in the yellow light of bad weather. Chain link borders the scrappy yard. My mother's childhood home?

I flip to a Polaroid of teenage Sidonie in a very early-nineties prom dress, in front of a tall brick building with *Fitchburg High School, Home of the Red Raiders* emblazoned on a sign. Her dress is long and straight and silvery, with a ruffled bit draped over her breasts like a curtain valance. Her date stands behind her: a tall black teenager with the kind of high pillar of hair I recognize from nineties TV shows. The tip of her head comes up only to the padded shoulders of his navy suit. Even though she's awkward in the picture, elbows away from her body, pink-lipsticked smile showing all the wrong teeth, he looks thrilled to be with her. His grin is huge, and his hand rests lightly on her arm, like if he couldn't touch her he wouldn't believe his luck.

The last and latest is Mom, pregnant in the shade of a birch tree, in front of a gray stone fountain I recognize from the Patty Linden Memorial Park in Sugarbrook.

Clutching the photos, I want to say, Great, this helps; here's my number and thanks for your time. I'll make my way out of this dim apartment, which *is* weird—pickles-in-your-desk-drawer weird. I wasn't expecting Lil to bake us scones or break into "Be Our Guest," but if she couldn't have been happy to see me, she might've been . . . interested? Instead of acting like her estranged cousin's daughter is some Girl Scout selling charity magazine subscriptions to support underage monkeys or cure albinism.

Jessa stands up from the table, which is my ticket to ride. But when I open my mouth, the one question I've wanted to ask all along bubbles out. "Did she ever ask about me?"

Lil's whole face slides downward just a bit, but she clamps her jaw and tightens up. "Last time we talked, she never said much about anyone but herself."

I wish I knew what Lil was thinking. Sherlock Holmes would know. On the one hand, that guy is bug nuts—he's selfish, rude, and messy. He leaves beakers and pipettes and knives and poisoned shoe polish lying all around. Sometimes Watson wakes up to find Holmes watching him from the foot of the bed at five a.m. He solves a lot of mysteries after sulking on the couch in his sitting room for days. Confession: when I read *A Study in Scarlet*, the first book about Sherlock Holmes and his lifelong sidekick, Dr. John Watson, I paid particular attention to the scene where Watson walks in to find Holmes on his back, staring with dulled eyes at the ceiling of No. 221B Baker Street. Dad did the same in the bad times, a few of which I'd seen before we went to Lindy, and I thought maybe it was because that was how *he* figured out his mysteries. So Dad needed a little help sometimes—so what? Holmes needs Watson, and not just to fetch his shoes or write his biography. Watson brings him cases to solve when he's been sitting around for weeks shooting morphine and cocaine. Watson's the keeper of all the knowledge Holmes considers beneath him—literature, philosophy, politics. He didn't even know the Earth revolved around the sun till Watson told him so, for god's sake.

But flaws aside, Sherlock Holmes can read people like no other detective. He spent his whole life studying regular people instead of learning how to become a regular person. When he meets Watson, he knows the guy has been an army doctor in Afghanistan by the stiffness of his arm, the tan on his face, and the paleness of his wrists.

I look at Lilian Eugene and try to read her life.

Once she had a husband. Now she lives alone, and if she has coworkers or boyfriends or girlfriends over to visit, there sure isn't any evidence around her apartment. Lil didn't even have a second chair set out before Jessa and I came, and there are pictures of no one anywhere, unless you count a Garfield calendar tacked up by the wall phone. I think of how she sat on the kitchen floor with her babies, though it physically hurt her to do it. How her clothes were covered in their hair before they walked all over her, like she spends her whole life down there among them. I think of the bobblehead in her car, the Petco bags she lugs her school stuff and cleaning supplies around in, like she's got an endless hoard of them. The cats are absolutely everything to her, and she doesn't love them halfway; she loves them hard.

Once Lil had a cousin, and they loved each other enough that even after they lost touch, she was my mother's emergency contact, the one person Mom trusted to come if she was called. Maybe Lil loved Sidonie Faye hard, that little girl drawing creatures in the tent in Fitchburg, the girl she shared her family with. Then Mom slipped away, called her once for money and never again, and Lil closed all that love up and put it away like a book on a shelf. So I come around after all this time and she acts like we're strangers, even if we're connected by something as everything-and-nothing as blood. I almost wouldn't believe even that connection, except for Lil's chin, the tip of an aging heart.

"Okay. Thanks for your help, Lil."

"If I could tell you more, I would. But by the time she left your daddy, I didn't really know her anymore."

A stray thought stops me in the doorway. "Hey, did she ever say anything about marrying Dad? Whether they were, or were planning to, or anything?"

Lil looks surprised. "I guess I always thought they *had* gotten married. Like I said, we weren't close at all, not at that point. I was shocked she called me up when she left. But she did talk about getting married, once. In the beginning, when she first came back. Sid said she could see herself happy, and if she and your daddy tied the knot, she wanted to do it on the same date they'd met. Their anniversary, kind of. She thought it'd be romantic, on account of the holiday. I told her sure, though secretly I thought that was strange, because that was the same day she went to claim Siobhan's body."

"And that day . . . was it Valentine's Day?"

"Yes, 1995, that would've been." Lil blinks at me. "Why, that day mean something to you?"

NINE

It's not that my dad is superstitious, but . . . he does like
to find the meaning in things.

He claims it's because he tells stories. That it's
the job of a writer—even writers of popular medical
mysteries—to sift through random events and watch
patterns emerge, like finding constellations in a giant
star-speckled sky. Maybe that's why he doesn't write
during the bad times. He once said in a session with
Lindy that things seem meaningless in the bad times,
and how can he write if he can't find meaning?

In the spring at the very end of seventh grade, Dad

and I were brainstorming a place for our two-man family vacation. It was his idea, a "you survived middle school, now gird your loins for high school" adventure, he called it. We were at the Subway on East Main, in our traditional front corner booth farthest from the bathroom, eating our traditional Spicy Italian on flatbread and Chicken and Bacon Ranch Melt, which we enjoyed at least twice weekly. (Dad wasn't so much of a cook before Lindy came around.) On the greasy-skating-rink table, there was an ad for Subway's new Santa Fe Wrap. While we ate, Dad scribbled a list of possible places on the back of the ad. Niagara Falls, he said. The Grand Canyon, he said. Hawaii, I said, which he dutifully wrote down as: *Hawaii (yeah right)*. When our sandwiches were reduced to lettuce shreds he tucked the ad in his jacket and we headed out. We then proceeded to the parking lot, where we had to squeeze our slightly fatter selves around a Hyundai Santa Fe that'd parked too close to Dad's truck, forcing him to shovel me through the driver's side.

As we backed out, Dad braked to stare at the back of the Hyundai, then plucked out the Subway ad, and with an alligator clip he had me fish from the glove box, clamped it to his sun visor like a postcard. "What do you think, Immy? Santa Fe, New Mexico. Purple mountains? The Rio Grande? Big sunsets? Saloons? The Wild West!"

I buckled in. "Because of a sandwich wrap?"

"Because of a wrap *and* an SUV. *The stars are aligned.*"

"I don't know. . . ."

But that night on TV, the Pirates game Dad had wanted to watch was canceled for rain. So we turned on the DVD player, having neglected it for months, and up came the last movie we'd left in the machine: *Ace in the Hole.* As you may or may not know, *Ace in the Hole* is an awesome, twisty fifties noir about this drunk, disgraced big-city investigative journalist who has to go work for a crappy little paper in Albuquerque. Albuquerque, New Mexico.

Dad tossed aside the extra-butter popcorn we were splitting, and our platter of ham roll-ups (our family recipe—like Fruit Roll-Ups, almost as gummy, but made with prepackaged ham from the convenience store instead of fruit). He stood, spread his arms to the heavens, and shouted, "THE STARS ARE ALIGNED!" And so that summer we spent a week in Santa Fe.

We hiked Tent Rocks and ate ice cream made to look like baked potatoes at the Cowgirl and shopped for cheap art at the street market in Old Santa Fe. On the last evening before our ten a.m. flight home, while we perused the gift shop of our pink adobe motel for every kind of chili product available—from red chili jam to chili chocolate to chili-flavored soda—the cashier told us about this great, isolated lake in the foothills of the Sangre de Cristo Mountains. Though I was pretty sure we'd be captured by hill people, Dad was like, "Nah," so we set out in the late evening.

It was dark and cool when we got to Santa Cruz Lake. Beyond the parking lot was a squat beach and, reaching out into the water, a long metal dock. We clanked over the walkway to the end of the dock and spread out a blanket. The water was dark and pretty deep. It lapped gently at the dock maybe a foot below the platform, the *hush, hush, hush* of it the only sound forever. We lay back and tilted our faces up into a million stars you could never see from the suburbs. Instead of the Sugarbrook sky, filmy and gray with streetlights and stadium lights and neon signs, the sky out there was huge and dusty with limitless solar systems.

"See, Immy?" Dad said hoarsely. "The stars are aligned."

The very next book Dad wrote was *The Case of the Weeping Woman*. The plot had Miles Faye traipsing out to Santa Fe to help a cousin accused of drowning his girlfriend in Santa Cruz Lake. *Weeping Woman* went big, his biggest novel yet, and in interviews he said he was inspired by the universe, New Mexico, and Subway.

If we hadn't seen the ad for the Santa Fe Wrap. If the Hyundai Santa Fe hadn't parked so obnoxiously that we paid particular attention to it. If a mass of air hadn't cooled to its saturation point, condensing water vapor into clouds that poured rain on a ball field in Pittsburgh, leaving us no choice but to turn on the DVD player and find *Ace in the Hole*. For Dad there's some kind of mystical significance behind the ifs, playing one big cosmic game of connect-the-dots. Not god or anything. *Meaning.*

Even when I was little and playing literal connect-the-dots in my coloring books, it kind of seemed like bullshit. Whatever blocky shapes emerged from my crayon, they never really looked like flowers or balloons or boats. Just jagged approximations in purple wax.

What I'm thinking is: *Of course* there was a Santa Fe Wrap advertisement in our booth—we always chose that table because it was farthest from the bathroom. That meant it was closest to the front door, where every few minutes a customer would let in a blast of baking heat or biting cold, depending on the season, making it pretty undesirable to everyone but us, so whatever ads were plopped on the table before the breakfast shift likely stayed there past lunch. And duh, we passed a

Hyundai Santa Fe on our way out; it is, after all, a top safety pick. And sure, *Ace in the Hole* was in the player. It's one of our favorites; we once went through a snap where we watched it six times in a month. There's a reason for everything, if you look hard enough. An answer for every mystery.

If Dad met my mother on February 14 of 1995—the day he showed her the body of Siobhan Faye and gave her a stone heart, as much a twentieth anniversary as any for my I-now-know-unmarried parents—then Lindy was wrong about Valentine's Day meaning nothing to Dad, especially if he and Mom had ever talked about marrying. That day meant everything to him, even when nothing else did; I know because even in the bad times, he told me my bedtime story.

I'm on his trail. I've felt it all along, and if I wasn't 100 percent positive he was off trying to save my mother, I am now. This is proof, actual and undeniable. What's more, I think he left the heart for me not as a clue, but as a map. Hoping just this once I would see it too, the picture in the stars, and use it to find my way to him.

TEN

"*Why are you* doing that with your face?" Jessa winces at me while I lead us through the frosty parking garage.

"Doing what? I'm smiling."

"Yeah, but it's a crazy smile. Like you're gonna pour me tea and make me a hat."

"I just feel like I'm on the right path," I say, breathless with the body-slamming, finger-burning cold and with something else entirely. With this small balloon of excitement rising in my stomach.

"And you think this because . . . ?"

On the third level, I spot my Civic. We heave ourselves inside the car and I fumble to turn on the heat.

How can I tell her about Valentine's Day and the lie of my parents' marriage and stone hearts? About the stars and the constellations? I can't, not even close. "It's— hard to explain."

"Uh-huh."

She sounds dubious, but I'm only half paying attention as I ask myself what I *know*.

My mother grew up in Fitchburg.

My mother was good at art.

My mother was troubled waters, like her mother before her.

"Hey, you want to, like, take a break tonight?" Jessa asks. "I mean, where are we gonna go on a Sunday night, anyway? Just a little break. My parents are visiting my grandma, so the soccer team's coming over."

The soccer team she's talking about doesn't exist as an actual soccer team anymore. It's just a few guys from Chad's old team, the Sugarbrook Sandpipers, who went to Boston colleges. They hang out in his basement bedroom with beer, the WiiU, and the secretive scent of weed drifting off them.

Dad avoids social gatherings even in the best of times, and when I can't get out of them, I fulfill my very important duty of shoring up the wall. I fold my arms and cross my legs and try to find a cool position that communicates *I am perfectly happy jammed in my corner and have a lot of clever things to say, but there's no need to talk to me to make me prove it.* When the glittering Times Square ball dropped on the big screen at the Prices' New Year's Eve party last year, I was at the snack table with a pig-in-a-blanket in my mouth so it didn't look like I expected anyone, much less Chad Price, to make with midnight kisses.

"Um, possibly."

"Jeremy's bringing Yuengling just for me."

"That's gallant."

I hand Jessa the photos to hold, but flip through a few loose pages at the bottom of the pile. I unfold a brittle piece of butcher paper to find drawings in thick, dark pencil. As soon as I realize what they are, I tuck them into my coat pocket to pore over in private. This is a part of my mother I'm not ready to share.

The other item in the pile is safer, an exhibition brochure for the Boston Museum of Fine Arts. It looks old, the paper fingerprinted and thin. I'm not sure why it's in the stack—maybe a souvenir from when Mom worked there—until I skim the section on special exhibitions. There's a bit about a Masters of Fantasy show, the collected works of artists who "explored the worlds of the imagination, the inner reality of the subconscious, and of dream."

Above the caption is a shot of the exhibit.

"You're not listening to me, are you?" Jessa objects.

Had she been talking? "Yeah, okay, whatever. But first I need to see something."

Lindy is out when I get home. I knew she would be. She left a message on my phone that she had errands to run, and encouraged me to take a break from my marathon hangout with Jessa and stop home. Encouragement to the tune of "Imogene Scott, if you aren't sitting across the kitchen table from me in the next twenty-four hours, you'll be eating every lunch for the entirety of February break in my office at work."

Lindy's always given me my space, but I'm beginning to suspect she's losing patience.

It's just as well she isn't here; it would feel wrong to walk unapologetically into Dad's office with my stepmother around. Settling into his rolling chair, I turn on his computer and reach into my bag while I wait for it to boot up. My knuckles scrape against the rough rind of the stone heart. But it's not what I'm after, and I dig deeper.

I punch in the password, wondering if Dad meant it to represent Miles Faye, or my mother. I make up my mind when the desktop brightens and floods with the familiar background. I never paid much attention to the picture. Each time I snuck on to Dad's computer,

I was rushing against the clock. Now that I'm squint-
ing at it with my face inches from the screen, I see the
details of the painting. There aren't many—it looks like
a watercolor and ink done in gray, and it's all pretty
fluid. Black scrawls for clouds, a slightly grayer wash to
separate the rain-scratched sky from steely seas. Men in
flat-bottomed wooden boats haul up fishing nets, robes
billowing in what must be a strong, dark wind. Inside
the scribbled nets, the shapes of fish like small sea monsters.

Pulling out the old Boston MFA brochure, I open it
to the prints and drawings section and flatten it on top
of Dad's desk calendar. There it is: the young woman
examining a framed work of art on the wall, awe in her
eyes. It's a gray picture of men in little wooden boats
hauling up full-to-bursting fishing nets before the storm
hits.

The young woman in the picture is my mother.

I have a stone heart, a scrappy backyard in Fitchburg
where my mother used to draw monsters, a Western
Union in Connecticut, a twentieth anniversary, and now
this: an inky sketch of fishermen. I don't know what it
adds up to, but I know it leads somewhere. And how do
I know that?

Faith. In Dad, and in mysteries.

I'm floating so high on that hope that when Jessa

calls, I forget how awkward and uncontrollable parties can be, especially parties with boys, and tell her sure, I'll come over, I'll come hang out with Chad and the soccer team, count me in.

By the time Jessa and I descend into the Prices' basement, the sort-of-party is under way.

On a pair of beanbag chairs in front of the TV, Chad and his old teammate Omar Wolcott lean into their Wii Wheels as they steer Bowser and Wario across the rickety bridges of Shy Guy Falls.

At the Ping-Pong table, Jeremy slaps a ball across the net to Mike Wazchowitz, who whiffs it. Jeremy gives Jessa a head-jerk nod while Mike scrambles around for the ball under Chad's plaid blanketed pullout bed.

Down on the floor, Omar does a cramped victory dance, constricted by his beanbag. Chad drops his controller, groans, turns, and sees us. He blinks, and I swear so does the silly, bloody muscle in my chest.

"Look at you, Imogene," he says.

I blush and tug down my dress. "Yeah, look at me."

I had a pretty specific idea of what I wanted to wear tonight, but nothing right in my closet, so after walking to Jessa's through a cold, spattering rain, I borrowed from her: a minidress with swirls of lace over a silver slip. Because it was "retro," according to Jessa, tight on top and sort of triangled out at the bottom, the loose fit in the waist and hips meant I could wedge myself in. The hem of it barely reached my palms when I held my arms straight for inspection, so Jessa gave me a pair of thick pink tights. She was thrilled I was letting her play life-size Barbie for a simple basement party, and never asked the reason. It's not that I don't like makeup and heels, or girls who wear makeup and heels. I'm on board with third-wave feminism and whatever. It's just, it feels as if girls like Jessa, women like Lindy, had some kind of how-to-be-pretty handbook passed to them that was never passed to me. True, Dr. Van Tassel couldn't teach Jessa about dresses and mascara any more than Dad could teach me. But I remember the afternoon she enlisted her glamorous sister, Annette, who works for some glittery boutique on Newbury Street. She arrived with armfuls of *Cosmo*, a caboodle of lipstick. "Red lipstick can be ladylike," she said once Dr. Van Tassel had fled Jessa's bedroom, "but it can also be a great 'Fuck you, world!'" I left before the lesson began; Dad was taking me to the Friendly Toast that night.

Then there was Mrs. Patel, who let us try on makeup at her daughter Lavender's twelfth birthday sleepover. Perched on the rim of the Patels' Jacuzzi tub in the master bathroom, we passed around jeweled eye shadows and disks of blush and lip glosses like tubes of cake icing. The next morning, our cotton pillowcases were like pale faces, imprinted with red lips, violet eyelids, rosy cheeks. When I turned mine over for washing, Dad, who was in a rare mood, laughed and called me Madam de la Scott for the rest of the day. *Would Madam de la Scott desire her juice in le plastic cup or in le crystal champagne flute?*

In eighth grade Mrs. Botstein took a little group of us shopping before Danica's bat mitzvah, and though Danica's the kind of girl pained by a teacher's attention, under her mother's spotlight she glowed. "Try these boots," Mrs. Botstein said. "Oh, look at this! What about this blazer? Look at my daughter," she said, stepping back. "Isn't she just blossoming?" At which Danica blushed and the rest of the girls giggled, but I didn't.

Mrs. Tuzzi with her yoga body is only a size up from Katie, both of them short and small-boned with doll feet, and they switch off jackets and shoes with the speed of a pit crew changing tires at the Indy 500.

Ms. Nelson gave Shalmar her wedding necklace to wear to junior prom. Shalmar fingered the crooked pink pearls while we stood by the punch bowl, her nose so high in the air she'd have been the first to die in a fire.

Last Thursday, for Valentine's Day, Mrs. Rivers gave Jaime a school ring that belonged to her own mother, who'd died of breast cancer when Jaime was seven.

I don't like how it makes me feel to think of these things.

But I'm grateful for one thing: at least I have Jessa, and she has the manual dexterity of a stylist. I described to Jessa the exact updo I wanted, and asked for an eighties-style pink lip, which I do not wear. I sat at the little silk-covered bench at her vanity as she fiddled with my slippery, winter-static hair, leaning my head back into her hands and telling Jessa about the brochure.

"Huh. Fishes. So what next?"

"I don't know. I was thinking of going to the museum?"

"Cool. This is kind of exciting, right?" She scraped the last bobby pin over my scalp and cradled my chin with light fingers to do my lipstick.

"Exciting?" I mumbled open-mouthed.

"Yeah. Like, not that we don't know where your dad is. But looking for him and following clues and stuff? It's like we're really doing something."

"I guess I know what you mean."

"So do you want to do this stuff when you grow up?"

"When I grow up?"

"Or whatever, say you went to BU and you graduated and got a dog and now you're thirty and fabulous. What are you doing?"

I squinted as she tugged back the hair at my temples. Normally I'd give Jessa the line I use on Mr. McCormick, and Lindy, and whoever reads our self-important college application essays: I want to write great mysteries. But that's not really true. It's not whodunits of my own making that I want to solve; it's *the* mystery I've been waiting and reading and preparing all my life to unravel. Rather than spill my hopes and dreams all over Jessa, I dodged the question. "Who says I want to go to BU? It's enormous. I still get lost at Sugarbrook High sometimes, and that's just a big horseshoe. And I'd maybe run into Jeremy."

"He's not that bad," she insisted, not for the first time.

"Okay, so where do you want to go to college?"

"I *want* to go to RISD. They have all these computer art programs. Like graphic design?"

That made sense. Jessa liked art class best of all, was really good at it, and any job that required competence with a keyboard, she'd kill at.

"But I'll probably only get into, like, Quinsigamond Community College. I'm not like Chadwick."

"So he's smart? You're smart, Jessa."

"Pshh."

"You are! You're a better liar than me, right? So maybe you should be the writer."

"Or I should be a powerful fucking *wizard*. Voilà!"

I turned to face the mirror for Jessa's big reveal. The hair was right—a poofed-up kind of French twist in the back, with two thick braids wrapped around the crown of my head. Jessa can do anything with hair. And with the bright pink lips and a slick of liquid eyeliner, I looked . . . not exactly like the girl in the prom photo, with her curtained silver dress and braided French twist and winged eyeliner, but not unlike her either. The awkwardness of my elbows and knees helped as I tried to figure out what to do with my body. And my face really was shaped like hers—you could see it when our hair was up like this.

Jessa popped into the mirror behind me. "Hot! Chadwick's gonna want to rip your tights off like wrapping paper."

"Oh, whatever," I said, and then, "Doesn't he have that girlfriend, anyway? I thought he was still dating that girl. The ski instructor. That he brought home for Thanksgiving?"

She shrugged mysteriously and finger-combed her own hair. "Not that I know of."

It turns out there aren't any college girls or ski instructors at the party, but then there aren't usually, and calling it a party is pretty generous. What it is, is a collection of

Doritos bags, KFC buckets, beer bottles, and boys. Still, I know girls who would wear uncooked sausage links to this gathering of snack foods if it meant they could come. Soccer is big at Sugarbrook, and Chad, Omar, Jeremy, and Mike led the team to States, which made them übermensches. I mean, Chad was kind of a nerd off the field—all AP classes, the hardest science and math courses Sugarbrook offered, and a member of the tech club off-season. But I once saw Jaime Rivers fish his Slurpee straw out of the cafeteria trash and carry it around in her pencil case because it'd touched his lips.

Chad levers himself up with much squeaking of vinyl and shifting of beans. Clearly he did not spend an hour and a half agonizing over his outfit; he's wearing generic dark boy-jeans (wearing them well) and a white T-shirt with a huge blue jellyfish pumping across the front, a bowl trailing ribbons and clouds. On the back it reads *Rhizostome or Die*. His hair stands in damp spikes from a recent shower, paler blond under the basement fluorescents like a tangled halo.

Jeez.

He lopes over to us, then joins us by the mini fridge. On top is a small collection of liquor bottles and soda bottles, some of which he mixes into a red Solo cup while I relearn the freckles on his biceps I've spent summer days memorizing.

Jessa drives an elbow into my hip before heading for the Ping-Pong table.

"What are you drinking?" I ask. *So* clever.

"Just a Captain and Coke. Kind of heavy on the Captain." He hands it to me to taste, and our fingers brush. "You'd like it."

I take a long sip of it, sweet and syrupy and throat-burning.

He snatches it back. "When you're a grown-up like me. Stick with beer and gather ye rosebuds while ye may, youth."

"I'm not that youthful. *You're* not that old."

"You are," he says, laughing, "one year and four months younger than me. That's more than the lifespan of the brine shrimp. That's, like, one brine shrimp and one dragonfly. That's fifteen bees younger! And there's this mayfly—"

"It lives for an hour, right? It has no mouth and no digestive system and it's made to have sex and die." I stifle the urge to crack my knuckles. "Just like college boys."

The dimple in his left cheek appears. "So you watch Animal Planet. So what? Young people watch Animal Planet."

"Not many."

"You're still . . . 10,958 mayflies too young for the

Captain." Then, squaring himself to me—the toes of his socks inches from my mine, his dimples at eye level, and his green eyes warming my face—he places his palm on top of my head, measuring. He lifts it and hovers it just above, so I can still feel my hair catching on his callused skin. My whole scalp tingles.

Chad grins. "Must be this tall to ride."

"Ride what, *Chadwick*?" Jessa squeezes past us, Jeremy on her heels. She looks cool and slick in a long white tank top and electric-blue leggings, and Mike Wazchowitz misses an easy volley at the Ping-Pong table when she bends over to look in the fridge.

Clearing his throat, Chad turns on her, blushing to the bright blond roots of his hair. "Mind your business, *Jenessa*." He stalks off and plops back in the beanbag with his drink.

As Jeremy pours two cups, she twists her hair into a red-gold rope, then releases it, the strands winding apart, spreading out, shining. Her smile is a white slice in the dim basement.

Jeremy hands her the drink and asks what I want.

"Captain and Coke, please."

He lifts both eyebrows.

This is the point in the evening where I'd usually pick a spot and commence leaning against the wall with a beer and a powdery handful of Doritos until Jessa swept Jeremy up and away to the Damon Salvatore side of the bed. Then I'd retreat to the snowy quiet of outside and walk the ten minutes home alone, safely feeling my feelings. But I did come dressed to kill, so instead of doing that, I take my drink and sit on Chad's bed to watch the Ping-Pong game. I decide to fake it till I make it. (This is one of Lindy's big Tips for a Happier, Healthier Family. "Positive action can open the door to positive feelings," she would say. "Put your sneakers on instead of your slippers, your jacket instead of your bathrobe." On Dad's first real date with Lindy, he wore his tux.)

Even though I don't especially care about the Ping-Pong match, and I suspect the guys don't especially care if I care, I root Jeremy and Mike on in turn. They aren't terrible, and the more I sip my Captain and Coke, which tastes stronger than Chad's, the more intense the game seems, the funnier the ambitiously failed swings, the more dazzling Jessa and Jeremy are, with his hand in her back pocket, her breast on his biceps, their mouths darting together and flitting apart like dragonflies (nearly four of which I am younger than Chad). After my second cup, handed to me by Mike on his way back from the mini fridge, I think I'm doing a pretty good job of making it.

When I'm quiet and still for too long at parties, I start looking for ways to slip out—I have that in common with Dad—but tonight, I'm committed. So when that starts, I leave the bed to watch Chad and Omar play Mario Kart. They offer me a controller, and Chad smiles over his shoulder at me during a break in the action. Though my eyes are zooming in and out of focus a bit, I'm hotly aware of his teeth, very white, and my own teeth, marginally dull from childhood braces. I bet the Prices brush their perfect teeth with bottled water when I'm not around to shame them into using the tap. Did I brush my teeth before the party? Do I have lipstick on my teeth? Does my breath smell like Doritos? Does Chad's? No—when I lean in toward the TV, he smells like boy. Like plaid flannel sheets and spicy deodorant and socks that aren't unclean, per se, but might've been hibernating under the bed for a week before he found them and pulled them on, because socks are socks to a guy like Chad. I respect that. I funnel my third drink into my mouth during a break in the game to stop myself from leaning in farther and whispering something "witty" about socks into his perfect seashell ear. He lists heavily to the left as he tries to make a hairpin turn around a penguin, then winces as the unstoppable Wario and immovable penguin collide nonetheless. I like the way he tries to steer with his whole body. I like the way he flinches when he crashes, as if in actual, 3D pain. I like the way he exists—another thought I close my lips around to keep from whispering.

Jessa unravels from Jeremy and drops down on the rug beside me. "I'm glad you're having fun, Im," she coos, her syllables dragging slightly.

When Omar loses for the sixth (sixteenth?) time, he suggests we play kings, which I'll later remember in flashes:

Jessa pulling nine, make a rhyme, surprising us all with a win by rhyming "telescope" with "artichoke."

Chad insisting we girls stick to beer, but being a little too far gone himself to check our cups closely.

Mike drawing eight, invent a rule, after which Jeremy has to sip every time anyone shouts, "Douchebags drink!"

Chad, his comet-white teeth and his deep, rumbly voice.

Jessa linking her arm through the hot crook of my elbow, and me feeling so good that I let her.

Me, pulling the fourth and final king. Omar hands me the center cup, where a mixture of Sam Adams and Captain and Coke and at least a little tequila and who knows what else swirls in one dangerous mud-brown brew. "Guys, no way, no way," Chad says, and tries to relieve me of the cup.

"Let her do it, Chad," Jeremy says. "She needs a good time right now, you know?"

Chad asks us what he means.

"Because of—" Jeremy looks at Jessa, pale between us, and then at me. "Because of your dad being lost, right?"

I turn to the wavering faces around the circle. Mike and Omar are watching me like I'm a bucket of water about to tip. And Chad. Chad is the worst of all.

I cough the terrible mixture down, throw the cup back, then trip up the basement stairs, through the Prices' perfect, shiny kitchen. Jessa's slurred voice shouts my name from below, but through the spinning of the world on its strange new axis, I consider the time it will take her to stand, let alone crawl up the steps, and time is on my side. Pausing just long enough to make my unsteady hands, which no longer seem to belong to me, pick up my purse and coat, I spill out onto their lawn.

Even in winter and in the dark, their grass seems painfully green.

ELEVEN

At eleven a.m. on the fifth day after my dad goes missing, I sit down on a bench at the Boston MFA, trying not to throw up on my sneakers.

The squeak of winter boots on white tile floors, the echo of a man lecturing his wife on postmodern art, the bleats and barks of kids who've had culture forced upon them on their school vacation—all of it boils over in my brain. My stupid brain, which feels like a cracked egg. I drop my face into my hands and try to ignore the nausea I've been swimming in since I woke up this morning to the chiming of Jessa's relentless texts, all of which I ignored, switching my phone to merciful silence. I was still in Jessa's dress. My carefully braided hair was a ruinous heap, now scraped snarls-and-all into a bundle at the back of my throbbing head.

I've seen Dad hungover. I know some of the tricks. Like, there's a sleeve of low-fat saltless Ritz in my bag, smuggled out of Lindy's diet cabinet in the pantry. And I've been guzzling water since I woke up; I stuck my face in the fountain by the museum bathroom until a mom behind me tapped her foot on the floor and muttered, "Leave some for the fishes."

Dad's hangover ritual, other than flavorless carbs and sleeping till two under an Everest of blankets, is a single drink first thing in the morning. Once, he had this book party in Boston that he was contractually obligated to go to. This was just pre-Lindy, at the start of the last real bad time, and his agent had to put him in a two-hundred-and-something-dollars late-night cab ride home. Dad called me from the front steps so he could use me as a crutch to the sofa. The next morning, I watched him make a tall Bloody Mary, sweating and gray-faced. "Don't breathe so loud, Immy," he begged me. "I'm recovering."

"From being drunk?" I stage-whispered.

"From waking up."

Unfortunately, Lindy was still around when I

dragged myself out of bed this morning, and it was all I could do to keep my game face on when we passed each other in the hallway. "It's a beautiful morning," she chirped, though it was a hollow, preoccupied kind of joy, like an underpaid Starbucks barista might offer. Still, she probably would've noticed me mainlining vodka and Tabasco.

I prop my chin up on my fist and stare at the painting across from me. A porcelain-pale woman hefts a baby boy. She's supposed to be the Virgin—I've never been to church or anything, but the cloak and tiny Bible give that much away—so I guess that makes her kid Jesus. Except since this is the Renaissance Art of Northern Europe and Italy wing, he's painted in that Renaissance style where it's obvious none of the artists took a child-development class. None of them understood the head-to-body proportions of a baby. Take Jesus, who looks like a grim-faced elf, with a long body and dangling sausage limbs and a head the size of a tennis ball. In all these paintings, it's as if the kids were never young; they were born miniature adults. Like instead of growing older, they just increased in length and height and weight. Which I bet would be a lot easier if it were true.

When the wave of nausea peaks and passes, I push myself to my feet and keep moving through the interconnected rooms. The museum map shows me where

I want to be, and after a few wrong turns I find the long room labeled Drawings and see it: just a little thing compared to the big art around it. Though my head is bobbing with the tiny boat in its inky water, I plant my feet and stare.

Beside the drawing, the plaque reads:

The Miraculous Draught of Fishes
Gift of the estate of Mrs. Sarah Wyman Whitman
through Mrs. Henry Parkman; acquired June 1909
Artist: Eugène Delacroix, French, 1798–1863
Medium: Pen, brown ink, and washes on paper
According to the Gospel of St. Luke, Christ chooses the poor fishermen Simon, Peter, and Andrew as his first Apostles. They have been fishing unsuccessfully in the Sea of Galilee when Christ appears and tells Peter to let down his nets into deep water. They make a miraculous catch, so their boats overflow with fish. The tale of the fishermen has long been a popular subject among artists, many religious, but some with humbler motives. *The Miraculous Draught of Fishes* has been re-created by more than one painter living in poverty, poignantly expressing a starving man's wistful dream of plentiful food.

The fishermen's shadowed faces don't have much in the way of features, but they don't look awestruck or burning with god fever. The slashes of their lips are straight, their squiggly muscles straining to haul in the catch while dark clouds billow in from the left. They seem nervous, in a hurry to gather the fish before the storm hits and everything they have is washed away forever.

I'm leaning in as close as I can get to the canvas without bells or alarms or just a strained museum guide sounding off, when fingertips brush my arm from behind.

"I wasn't touching it!" I jump back, turning so fast it takes the room a second to catch up with me. But it isn't a museum guide.

It's Jessa.

"What the hell?" I press my hand against my thumping heart. "What are you even doing here?"

"Ugh, don't shout," she groans through dry lips. Now that my vision has refocused, she does look rough, a whole rainbow of unhealthy colors. Her skin is practically green, and there are purple smudges under her eyes, red-rimmed and bleary. She pulls at the strings on her oversize sweatshirt, drawing the hood in like a noose. "Morning-me is really not feeling night-me. I thought I was gonna upchuck the whole train ride."

"You took the train in?"

"Well, yeah. You wouldn't text me back. Then I went to your house and saw your car was gone, so I got Chad to drop me off at the station on his way to work. And it was *horrible*. I'm not even kidding. The lady next to me was eating this sandwich out of a paper bag, so I asked if I could borrow the bag, you know? Just in case? And she gave me the stink-eye like I tried to rob her. Like, I was just *asking*."

"And you've been wandering around trying to find me?"

She shrugs. "I just asked someone in a vest about a fish picture."

"Oh. I guess that would've been easier. . . ." I turn back to the drawing on the wall.

"Any clues here?" Jessa asks.

"Not so much." Swallowing back a swell of nausea—maybe I've been staring a little too closely into the rolling waves of *The Miraculous Draught of Fishes*—I make for the bench in the middle of the room and collapse onto it, trying to tell myself this isn't the end of the trail. It's just the part in the mystery when the answers seem really far away; the depressing part that makes it all the more inspiring and kickass when the detective picks up the trail again. But I'm a little too hungover for that bullshit. "Being here just . . . helps me think," I finish lamely.

"I'm really sorry," she mumbles, "about telling Jeremy. When you and Chadwick were busy measuring each other, Jeremy was whining about me not spending any time with him on my break. Because he wanted me to go to this college thing with him today, but I said I was helping you with something really serious, and he should shut up about it. And then he was like, 'Is it *herpes*?' He was being such a tool and I wanted him to feel like a tool, so I told him the truth. I shouldn't have, but I didn't think he'd blab to the entire room and I'm so, so sorry. I'll talk to my brother. Tell him to forget about it."

"Whatever." It's out of the bag already, and it's too late to put it back. "Why are you going out with that guy if he's such a tool?"

She winces as a little girl across the room screams at a glass-splintering decibel, then sighs. "He's not always. Like last semester, when I was fighting with my mom a bunch? And freshman year, when my dad was having stomach problems? And we thought maybe he had, you know, the C-word or something, so Chad was applying to Boston schools only? Jeremy was so sweet. He was always coming around to play stupid video games and make Chad feel better, and me too. That's kind of when we started dating."

"What? I didn't know any of that."

"Your dad had just gotten engaged to Lindy and you were kind of blah about it. I didn't want to drag you down. You take things *really* seriously, you know?"

"Oh." That makes me sound like I really *am* a bucket of water about to tip. "I'm sorry you couldn't tell me about that."

"It doesn't matter. I know you care about me," she says, and then, "Hey, Im? I have a question, but don't get mad."

"Uh-huh?"

"Have you told Lindy what we're doing? What you think your dad is doing? I mean, maybe she would believe you."

"Why? Do you believe me?"

"Sure," she says, toying with her hair. "I guess. Like, I don't really *get* all these clues . . . but I'm not smart like you. And I don't know your dad the way you do, obviously," Jessa hurries to add.

"Right. You're just helping because you're my best friend." I pause to consider this. "You might be my only actual friend."

"That's not true," she says, but it's a pretty soft protest.

"Still, thanks, anyway. For helping. You know, Lindy wants to put up posters in Stop and Shop and all over. So if we don't track him down soon, everyone will find out."

"Is that such a bad thing? Like, you keep saying it's your job to find your dad. But I don't get it. You're not a detective. You're not a superhero. I don't remember you becoming, like, 'one with the night.' It is literally the police's literal job to find him. So shouldn't we tell the cops what we know? They could look up your mom's, I don't know, criminal record and stuff."

"Why would my mother have a criminal record?"

"Robbed a bank? Stole meatballs from Sweden? Who knows? No offense, Im, but it doesn't seem like your mom was the most . . . well-adjusted person in the world, right? If you're sure your dad's going after her, they can find them faster than we can."

She's probably right about the police. She's definitely right about my mom. But the thing is, I don't want her to *be found*. *I* want to find her. I stumble over my words to make Jessa understand.

"You mean you want to find *him*, right?" She frowns. "You mean your dad? 'Cause I thought that was the whole point. Find your mom because that's where your dad's headed."

"It was," I answer slowly. "But now . . ."

I want to explain to her that for other girls, a mother is a makeup lesson in the master bathroom, a set of pearls at junior prom, a handwritten letter every Valentine's Day. For me, a mother is a small body always out of frame in old photos. Just flashes of dangling hair, the toe of a shoe, the tips of outstretched fingers. A wistful dream of plentiful food. And it isn't enough to keep me going anymore. My mother is half of who I am, and I don't know her at all.

But the only way I can explain it is, "I just keep thinking about being in a room with them. Walking into, I don't know, a crappy little breakfast diner, the kind with a jukebox that only plays the old songs no one remembers, and seeing them at a booth, and then I go sit in the booth with them and . . . there we all are."

"Okay." Jessa speaks up after a long moment, saving me. "So we'll keep looking."

We sit quietly, watching a cluster of noisy preteen boys. They push each other and pull on each other's coats in front of a woodprint of a saint being stretched by his limbs between four men on ink-black horses. "Observe." I scowl at them. "The male of the species at play."

"Next comes the poop-flinging and penis-fencing."

I laugh even though the sound of it hurts.

I feel the last little wisps of anger go out of me as I remember a free period Jessa and I shared when we were both new in high school. It was in the school cafeteria, where all underclassmen spent their study halls. Early on we staked out the corner table behind the vending machines. Optimal territory for whispering, plus we could get a Vitaminwater whenever we wanted without having to ask permission. Partly because of the vending machines but mostly because Jessa has been gorgeous and perfect forever, freshman boys would circle our table like summer gnats. Matthew Biltz in particular had a five-hundred-ton crush on Jessa. With ears like teacup handles and a chronic case of BO (the consequence of an uncircumcised penis and frequent masturbation, Ashley Griffin was heard to speculate), he leaned on a mean sense of humor to get girls to look at him. He'd drift over to our table on the pretense of buying a SunnyD and, because he loved Jessa, he'd turn his mean on me to attract her. Slamming shut my trig textbook, tweaking my bra strap through my T-shirt, shooting rubber bands into my ponytail, pulling his eyes down and to the side like mine. Moves worthy of Casanova. He'd do this each free period until the day Jessa invited him to sit with us, to spread out his work so the supervising teacher would think we were studying together. The wattage of his smile could've powered an auto plant, until Jessa took a huge swig of Vitaminwater, leaned over, and emptied a warm and gelled mouthful right onto his classroom-issued copy of *The Merchant of Venice*. Matt used his spit-rippled book the rest of the semester, because what boy would dare complain and let it be known he'd been slapped down by Jessa Price?

I don't approve of book abuse. But he never bothered me again.

Jessa tips her head onto my shoulder. "Who needs boys, anyway?"

Resting my cheek on the top of her tangled hair, I try to smile. "Definitely not us." I tuck my hands into the pockets of my coat and feel the crunch of butcher paper.

"What is that?" Jessa asks as I pull out the folded drawings.

I figure it's time. Together, we peer down at a skeleton, a cloaked vampire, a bull-headed minotaur. Probably from Mom's how-to-draw books; she'd clearly tended toward the monsters. The lines are clean and confident, except for a shakier sketch of a girl among them. Her facial features are undecided upon, fingers and shoes unfinished. Scrawled in the bottom corner, in numbers that match Lil's handwriting on the Post-it Note: *Sidonie Faye, 1991.* Mental math tells me my mom was fourteen when she drew this . . . what would you call it, a self-portrait? I trace one finger over the still-greasy pencil of a werewolf's claws.

"She was really good," Jessa whispers.

"She was something," I whisper back.

"Okay, so . . . now what? We know your mom was working in an eye doctor's office five years ago, right? So we make a whole bunch of appointments in Connecticut?"

"No." I rise carefully from the bench with the beginnings of an idea. "But maybe we do need a grown-up."

TWELVE

"Come on, make one phone call in your big-boy voice," Jessa pleads through the white cloud of her breath. "It will take you two minutes, and then you can go back to teaching grown adults how to fall down a hill. Do it for Im!"

I inspect a piece of lint on the sleeve of my coat, unable to look Chad in the eye. The blurred memory of him over his playing cards, the sympathy on his face, makes my skin feel too tight.

"It's not like I don't want to help you, Imogene." He frowns, pushing off the hood of his jacket and stomping the heavy powder off his boots in the doorway of the lodge. He's just come off the Blue Triangle course at the Marple Slopes, a little more than an hour northwest of Boston.

The lodge seems crowded for a Monday, everybody in their bright zippered ski gear, swish-swishing as they raise their arms, clomping heavy-footed in their boots toward fake log tables. This is how other kids spend their February breaks: riding ski lifts up the slopes, inhaling Cokes and French fries, hurling soaked ski gloves at each other like nylon grenades. Chad guides us to a quieter spot by the garbage cans outside the Marple Grill. The smell of meat and sauerkraut curls around us, and though I thought the long drive had given me time to regroup, I press the back of my hand to my mouth. Jessa looks similarly grossed out. Raising a pale eyebrow wet with snow spray, Chad scoffs, "Not feeling so awesome, are you? Let it be a lesson. You go sailing with the Captain, sometimes you get thrown overboard. Next time, listen to me."

"Ugh, never mind, *Chadwick*," Jessa says, clearly wrestling her gag reflex under control. "Just please do it?"

"Can't you tell me why I'm lying on the job? Is this . . . is this about last night?"

"Chad, just leave it alone," Jessa cuts in, an

uncharacteristic growl in her voice.

Her brother trains his eyes on me and I lift my chin, bracing for more questions, for a repeat of last night's pity party. Instead he peels off his gloves and wipes a hand down his face, flushed from the cold. "What do you need me to say?"

If he's willing to let it go, so am I. More than willing. Gratefully, I tell him how on the drive over, Jessa looked around and found an optometrist's office called Lionel Sorbousek Eye Care in Torrington, Connecticut. It's the closest match to Lil's guess at my mother's former employer. And I explain my plan. "But we need a grown-up."

A familiar dimple punctuates his left cheek.

"I mean we need someone who *sounds* like a grown-up."

I follow him into the office off the ski shop while Jessa stands watch outside. Not that this is a high-risk mission. The young employees in the lodge seem more interested in sharing epic stories of their epic weekends than in whatever's happening in their third-rate ski slope's tiny back office. Chad sweeps aside a collection of giant slushie cups on the desk and sits in the rolling chair, reaching for the phone. "I'll put it on speaker, okay? Just keep quiet."

While he dials, I pull up a metal folding chair and

study my winter-chapped hands until a woman answers, "Lionel Sorbousek Eye Care, how may I help you?"

"Yes, hi, this is Bob White in HR at the Marple Slopes. I'm calling about an applicant for a job we recently posted. She has your office listed as a reference, but this would've been five years ago. Is there someone there who would've been her supervisor?"

"One moment, please," she answers, and peppy, bland music like you might hear in toothpaste commercials trickles over the line.

"How did you come up with this plan?" Chad asks in a stage whisper.

"I read it in a book." *A Shriek in the Dark*, in fact, the tenth in a series by popular medical mystery writer Joshua Scott.

"Im," he starts, louder now. "Last night, I didn't really—"

The music cuts off. "This is Dr. Sorbousek."

"Yeah, yes, hello." Chad drops his deep voice an octave so it's practically on the ground. He's not as good a liar as his sister, but he mostly gets the script right. "I'm calling in reference to one of your previous employees, Ms. Sidonie Faye."

"Sidonie? Haven't heard that name in a while."

"She's applied for a job at our resort, and I was hoping you could tell me a little about Ms. Faye."

"She did work for us for, oh, about two years. She was a hard worker. Polite."

"So you didn't terminate Ms. Faye's employment? Because her resume mentions unusual circumstances, but it's a little fuzzy on that point."

"She wasn't fired, no." Lionel Sorbousek sounds taken aback. "In fact, I told her if she found herself back in the area after she settled her business, we'd try to find a place for her."

"Uh-huh," Chad says, watching as I dig a pen and pizza coupon out of the junkyard that is the desktop and jot a quick note. He squints at my handwriting. "Did she quit for any particular reason?"

Dr. Sorbousek hesitates. "Mr. White, I'm not sure I can say any more. Policy, you know?"

While Chad fakes a dramatic cough to buy time, I scribble a longer note and nudge the pizza coupon across the desk. Chad shakes his head no. I shake my head yes. He frowns. "I understand the position you're in, Dr. Sorbousek, but you have to understand the position *I'm* in. Ms. Faye will be working in the children's center, and will at times be responsible for the safety of a large number of children. Should she prove . . . not up for the task, I don't want us or anyone else to be liable. You're her most recent job listed, and the conditions of her leaving are vague. Any insight you could give me would be very much appreciated."

The doctor clears his throat. "There's not much I can tell you. She was quiet, but she did the job. Showed up regularly for work. Then one day she didn't, and called to say she'd gone back home for good. Said it was where she needed to be. I assumed it was a family matter. I told her we understood, and we were sorry to lose her. And I didn't hear from her again after that."

Three sharp knocks on the office door startle us: Jessa's warning.

While we've been listening to Lionel Sorbousek, Chad and I have both crowded around the phone, heads nearly together, breathing the same breaths. Now, Chad shoves his chair backward. "Thanks so much for your help, doctor. We'll, uh, take all of this under advisement." He rushes to hang up, then shuffles around in the bottom desk drawer. The two of us are seated a respectable distance from each other when the door swings open and a muscular girl in a blue Marple Slopes T-shirt strolls into the office.

"Busy?" she stops and asks.

"What's up, Pari?" Chad says.

The girl—Pari—crosses to the desk and props her elbow on his shoulder, her body resting against his arm. The tips of her fingers brush his chest, and one blue-black side braid dangles by his ear. Chad doesn't lean into her, but he doesn't shrug her off or roll away.

"Who's this?" she asks. Her eyes are perfectly round, dark mirrors.

"Im. Imogene Scott." He hands me a form he's pulled from the drawer. "She's applying to be a ski instructor."

News to me. I sit straighter and flick my chin up as she looks me over, from my tangled clump of hair to my shapeless puffy coat to the chubby legs inside my rumpled jeans. I resist the urge to crack my knuckles.

"Imogene . . . that's a pretty name," she settles on.

"Isn't it gorgeous?" he says, and lingering awkwardness aside, I can't help but flash my teeth at him.

"Do you guys know each other from somewhere?"

"Since forever. She's Jessa's friend."

"Your little sister?" Pari's eyes clear. "So you must go to high school, Imogene. Aww!"

Poisonous steam heats my cheeks and hisses in my ears. This is surprising, to say the least. Chad's had lots of girlfriends. I never felt jealous (not very, anyway) because whatever tricky feelings I was feeling, at least I was relieved of any responsibility to act on them. And now, in the middle of my search, is so not the time to act. But I can feel my smile shift, widen, and ice over into a smile that Jessa has trademarked. She calls it the Sweetest Bitch, usually reserved for the girls who whisper *slut* behind her back in the second-floor bathroom.

"Yup, I'm in high school. You must be, like, *hundreds* of bees older than me, Pari."

Chad stifles a laugh while Pari's whole face clouds over. So she's older and has biceps like basketballs and is presently draped across Chad. I've won some kind of girl-on-girl victory, and I take it with me when I leave.

Just beyond the office door, Jessa waits. "What'd you find out?"

I glance over my shoulder. "That I don't like Pari."

"Pari Singh? Why? She's so cool. She can, like, ski the Black Diamond slope backward, Chad says."

"Probably not that smart, though."

"No, she's *so* smart. She's studying weather-ology."

"So? What else does Chad say about her? Is she *the* ski instructor?"

Smiling, Jessa sucks her bottom lip. "How's it taste, those sour grapes?"

"There's nothing wrong with my grapes. She's just, she's all, ugh."

"Then why don't you do something about it?"

"About what?" I stuff the application into the Marple Grill garbage can, atop half-eaten logs of bratwurst and a soggy pile of cooled sauerkraut. As if I could work here. Dad has never brought me skiing. Too taxing for his couch-and-bathrobe times, too calm for his wander-the-unfamiliar-peaks-of-New-Mexico-at-midnight times. Not that I've begged him to go. I'm honestly grateful. On the long list of things I'll never do, tossing myself off a cold mountain is tied with setting my bookshelf on fire, skinny-dipping in a tank of rhizostome jellyfish, and confessing my love to Chad Price. "It's not important, anyway."

I bring Jessa up to speed on what *is* important as we shove our way out of the lodge, into a wind that carries crystals of snow and shatters them against our cheeks. At least the cloud cover's lifted, so the snowy hills of the Marple Slopes are bright and blue-lit, though in the east you can already see the sunset smoldering. Where has the day gone? Where have the five days since Dad's been absent gone?

Jessa takes small crunching steps toward the parking lot in her inappropriately fashionable boots. She swore she would've worn her boring boots if she'd known I would drag her up a mountain. "So your mom went home. To Sugarbrook?"

"Obviously not." I frown. Impatient with Jessa's stutter-walking, I plow forward only to slip on a glistening patch of snow. I feel myself tilt and fall, but Jessa throws out a hand and catches my elbow.

"Maybe he meant *home* home, Im. Like, all the way home."

"Which is—"

"Fitchburg." She grins, towing me forward by the arm until I get my feet back under me. "So why don't we go to Fitchburg?"

I will tell you why we do not go to Fitchburg. We don't go to Fitchburg because:

1) The sun is sinking fast out of the sky, about to extinguish itself against the already-dark horizon, and if another dinner passes at 42 Cedar Lane without me, I'll be eating lunch in Lindy's office in Framingham from now until next Monday.

2) I've stumbled on a problem that never seems to stop detectives in books: teenage poverty. Whatever shallow pool of money I made last summer working as scoop girl at the Frozen Gnome has dried to mud in the bottom of the creek bed that is my savings account. Dad is usually pretty reasonable with the money-lending, but he isn't here, and driving back and forth across Massachusetts to find him has wiped me out.

I turn down multiple offers from Jessa to fill my gas tank on the way home, because while it's great to have her with me, I'm not looking for a financial backer. Instead I do the only thing I can. I go *home* home.

My stepmother is back from work and reading in Dad's armchair in the living room. Pilates-thin and only a little taller than me, Lindy's swallowed by the hulking red seat, the chair back looming above her like an open mouth. It goes with nothing in the living room, otherwise a collection of almost-matching wood and two couches so old that most of the paisley's worn off. We've had them forever. Since I was little kid, at least. I don't remember a time without them. Most of our belongings are permanent in this way. The dancing-banana magnets on the fridge, the leather padded weights bench in the basement, the little potted plant that would be a towering oak by now if it weren't plastic. Lindy's managed a few changes—now we keep our flour and sugar in fancy little canisters instead of rubber-banded bags—but Dad and I like it the way it is. It's right the way it is, chipped paint, butt-bowed cushions and all.

The most recent addition to this house, besides my stepmother, is Dad's chair. He and I dragged it home from a yard sale five blocks over a few years ago. Dad had gone on new meds and was a little jumpy, so he wasn't supposed to drive just yet. But that couldn't stop us. We hauled it back on foot, knees knocking against the steep sides of the chair, fingers slipping, sweat spackling our faces.

"This is why you're my strongest girl yet," he told me.

I pause in the doorway and Lindy takes her time looking up from the book, though from the way she drops it shut without bothering to mark her page, I suspect she's been 49 percent reading a biography of Cleopatra, 51 percent waiting for me to walk in.

"Gosh, Immy, is that you? The boss has been making you work double shifts again, I take it? How's your 401k coming?"

"Okay, okay, I get it, I've been scarce."

"You've been absent," she says, and sighs. "But I get it too."

I scratch an itch on my ankle with one sneaker. I don't want to talk, to pretend I'm as lost as Lindy. But the situation calls for more than "Hi, how've you been, can you lend me a hundred bucks for mysterious purposes, maybe see you Tuesday!" Instead I land on, "It's fine. I'm fine."

She crosses to the couch and spreads her palm out on the cushion beside her.

"Right now?"

"Please."

I perch on the arm at the far side of the couch, examining my reflection in the darkened windows.

"How's Jessa?" Lindy asks.

"She's . . . Jessa. She texts. She talks a lot."

"What did you two do last night?"

I swallow the unpleasant memory. "Just hung around. Played Ping-Pong."

Lindy nods; I see it in the window, and Dad's old,

pilled bathrobe wrapped around her instead of the usual cape or kimono robe. "She's a good friend to you."

"Yeah, I know."

"Did the Prices feed you already?" she asks, maybe a smidge jealously.

"I wanted to eat with you," I say, which pleases her.

I follow Lindy into the kitchen to help with dinner, though there isn't much for me to do. My stepmother is as efficient a cook as she is a counselor. Before she starts on the ginger pork stir-fry and mashed veggie-of-the-week, she lines all her knives on the counter by size, her starches and oils by order of use, her vegetables by quantity (three-fourths cup carrots before one-half cup snow peas before one-quarter cup chopped onion and so on). I learned my craft from the Joshua Scott School of Cooking, which is so utilitarian we never used to close the chip bags; in fact, we'd lean them on their sides in the cupboards with their crinkly plastic mouths wide-open and pointed frontward so all we had to do was open a cabinet door and reach a hand in.

Now, I do what Lindy tells me to. Pour this, wash this, move over so I can do this. I try not to think of it as giving her what she wants so I can get something (gas money, a few more days of freedom to search). I try to think of it the way Lindy does: as a bonding exercise.

"It's awesome," I assure her when we're sitting at the

table with our full plates, ignoring the empty seat beside us, which only makes it emptier.

"The pork came out very tender, but I think I went overboard on the ginger."

This is kind of classic Lindy. It was a big part of therapy when we were briefly with her—celebrating victories and identifying opportunities. "You say you went to the grocery store today, Josh! That's wonderful. A great victory over your depression. Congratulate yourself! And maybe tomorrow you can do two things, like go to the grocery store *and* put the food in the fridge so Imogene doesn't come home to eight-hours-warm milk and iceless ice cream." I'm paraphrasing, of course. Mostly.

I've often wondered about the moment when Dad decided, That's the one for me forever. I've been told the story of how they started dating. We'd only been to three or four sessions with Lindy before Dad ran into her at the Thinking Cup in Boston and invited her to share his high-top table. ("I won't be billed for this, will I?" he'd joked lamely.) While their coffees cooled, they talked, and a week later, Dad requested a different family therapist. He must've wooed her hard, because it wasn't long after that she switched practices altogether, and Dad sat me down at a low-top table at Cheesy Pete's and gave me the Lindy Talk.

But what was it about Lindy, exactly? What convinced him to marry her when apparently (and mysteriously) he'd never even married my mother? I'm not saying Lindy isn't wicked smart, ambitious, and nice enough, with hair that shines like polished wood. I don't object to Lindy in any specific way. But Dad's kept *The Miraculous Draught of Fishes* as his desktop background for as long as I can remember, and I can remember three laptops back. How do you love someone that much, then propose to your family therapist?

And for maybe the first time ever, I wonder when Lindy looked at Dad and thought, That's the man for me. What convinced her to risk so much for him? What convinced her to stay?

I watch as it takes my stepmother two delicate bites to snip a quarter-size piece of watercress off her fork tines with her front teeth. What would she think if she knew that Dad and Mom were never married? Would she be pleased with her shiny new first-wife status? Suspicious of whatever truth is lurking beneath the lie, like me?

Would she shake her head and tell me I'm chasing ghosts? I remember Victory Island, and place my bet on the latter.

"So, Immy. Thinking about prom yet?"

That's a topic switch. "Should I be?"

She smooths a napkin across her lips, starting from the center and working toward the corners. "It's in June, isn't it? Do you have a date in mind?"

As if all I have to do is think of a guy, and one will appear. I'm about to shrug it off, but this gives me a window. "Jessa wants to look at dresses tomorrow, before all the good ones are sold out." I sigh and cast my eyes downward. "But I don't think I'm going."

"You've still got time to shop."

"No, I don't think I'm going to prom."

She clinks her fork onto her plate, eyebrows screwing together. "I won't say you should go. But that seems like a rash decision."

"It's not *rash*. It's practical. I don't even have a boy to take me." It sounds pathetic—I have to swallow a healthy dose of self-loathing to get the words out—but I know the answer that's coming.

"Oh, Immy, you don't need a *boy* to go to your prom."

"No, I guess not," I reluctantly admit, tracing gloomy squiggles in my mashed butternut squash. "But boys usually buy the tickets. That's how the school does things and it'll look weird if I do."

"That's ridiculous! Not to mention a complete throwback to the fifties. You just march in and buy your own ticket."

I snort. "Me and what trust fund?"

Confident that she's facing a problem she can solve, Lindy picks up her fork and digs back in. "Well, don't worry about that. How much are tickets?"

"Who knows. But first I have to buy a dress and shoes and . . . I don't know." Then, the clincher: "All so I can show up without a date?"

"Imogene Mei Scott, you need to realize that you're a strong young woman who is perfectly capable of having a great time *sans* male. Tell me what you need."

"Thanks, Lindy," I gush, my smile genuine.

"Of course." She pats my hand across the table, then clears her throat. "You know, while you were with Jessa yesterday, I spoke with Officer Griffin."

I look at her. She smiles. Weakly, but at least she's still wearing her work lipstick, and her hair is smoothed back in a French twist, so she looks more herself. "It's not—there isn't any information yet. But Officer Griffin thinks my idea of getting the media involved might be helpful."

"The media? What, like, newspapers? TV?"

"Both. She thinks the story could really get some traction considering your dad's well-known. To some, anyway. People could really pay attention. And the more people who pay attention, the greater the likelihood that someone will see something. It might help us find him, just in case he isn't heading back this way already."

"It's only been a few days. Can't we wait?" I stand. I can just see some Fox 25 reporter in her ice-cream-colored suit and plastic makeup, delivering the line: "A local mystery writer is now the star of his *own* mystery."

Lindy looks up at me, her eyes sharpening. I now see the veins in them, the swelling in the soft pink corners I've been ignoring all this time. "This isn't the kind of decision we should be putting off. You're not a little girl, Imogene. You have a crucial role in this family, and I want you to be part of these decisions. I need you with me, and I need you to understand."

"I know you're worried."

"You must be worried too, Immy, even if you won't admit it."

On the one hand, I can practically hear my shoulders creak under the weight of everything I know, and everything she doesn't. She looks so sad, with her swimming eyes. But on the other hand, knowing what Dad is up to when no one else does almost feels like a superpower. And isn't it? Sherlock Holmes is a morphine and coke addict and depressed as hell. Dirk Gently from *Dirk Gently's Holistic Detective Agency* is a fat gambler who was once arrested for psychically plagiarizing exam papers. Nero Wolfe from *Over My Dead Body* drinks like a fish during Prohibition, keeps track of his boozing by stashing the bottle caps in his desk. And Miles Faye: in ten books, he never once had an actual relationship, and every friend of his we hear about is a dead friend. All the great detectives are screwed up somehow, and those are just the men. But they have the truth. They have the big answer. Isn't that the best power there is?

But I couldn't tell Lindy the truth if I wanted; I don't have it yet. So I duck the question. "Even Officer Griffin said he was, like, in control of his faculties. That he knows what he's doing."

"You heard that?" She sighs and digs purposefully into her stir-fry.

I stand. Let her think it's too hard for me to talk about, if it will end this horrible conversation. "I just . . . I just want to go shopping with Jessa tomorrow. Is it okay if I go to bed early?"

"Of course, Immy. Of course. I'll leave you some cash tonight for an outfit, to start."

"Thanks." I give my plate a lazy rinse in the sink, jam it in the dishwasher, and retreat to my room.

Like the rest of the house, my bedroom contains the same stuff it always has. Same twin bed, same sunwashed blinds, same pictures on the hand-me-down desk. Every book I've ever read, even the bad ones. I wouldn't throw away a book any more than I'd toss a pet out on the street, if I'd had any pets since my ill-fated goldfish. *Rebecca* is currently being used as a coaster.

I flop onto the unmade bed and reach into my book bag, extracting my copy of *A Time to Chill*, the stone heart, and the stack of photos. All of these I tuck into my nightstand drawer, except for one picture: Mom on the lawn of her childhood home, in front of the forked paper birch, the chain-link fence, the queasy storm sky. On the drive home from the ski slopes, Jessa tried dialing Lil's number to get an address a couple times, but she never picked up, and she never returned our messages. So no help's coming from her.

I squint at the small white house behind my mother. An American flag dangles from the lamppost along the front walk, limp and greasy-looking. If there's a number on the door, I can't see it.

In the next picture of Mom and Lil, they stand on the lawn of the church, a steeple towering over them with a pale green roof. I pull my own laptop from the desk. Speaking of problems that never crop up in detective stories these days, where's a genius computer hacker when I need one? The main mystery-solver always has a friend they can go to and say, "Hey, Sullivan, the perp seems to have disappeared by the old town hall." Then Sullivan sits at the computer, cracks his neck, and with a little pitter-patter on the keyboard, he says "Okay, I've accessed the security footage for the past twenty-four hours from the bank across the street, and here he is going into the storm drain behind the Pretzel Shack!" A friend like that could, I don't know, break into the Fitchburg real estate records and find the Fayes' and the Wards' old addresses in a heartbeat.

My Watson is busy eating dinner with her own family up the road. So I've got work to do before I get her back tomorrow morning.

THIRTEEN

"*Since when are* you busy?"

Jessa sighs over the phone. "I know, I *know*. Sucks, right? I totally forgot. I promised Mom we'd have a girls' day before this big pediatric conference she's going to, and this is her only day off all week. She booked us a treatment for two at In Your Facial, that spa in Newton? And she paid ahead of time."

"Okay, I understand."

"I'm really, really sorry. Trust me, Im, I'd rather go to Fitchburg with you than get a candlelight couples' massage with my *mother*."

Pressing my free ear against my bedroom door, I can clearly hear Lindy down in the kitchen. Right about now, she'll be scanning the political section of the morning paper and eating her usual breakfast: one cup Greek yogurt, one hard-boiled egg minus the yolk, two cups basic black coffee. I've got ten minutes till she marches upstairs to pack her briefcase, pops her head in my room to say good-bye, and is out the door by eight forty-five. After which, I'd planned to pick up my partner.

Sherlock Holmes was never stymied by Watson's pedicure appointments. But Jessa has plans with her mom, and I can't judge her for that. I wouldn't even know how.

"No, it's completely okay. Of course you should go. I'll be fine on my own."

"Excuse you?" she scoffs. "You may *not* go to a strange city and knock on strangers' doors alone. You will so get kidnapped, and I won't know how to find you without you."

"I won't get kidnapped because I'm not a kid."

"Yeah, I'm pretty sure that's what everyone says before they get kidnapped. But hey, Chad can totally go with you! He's not working and he doesn't have class on Tuesdays."

"I'm not dragging your brother—"

"Chadwick!" she shouts into the speaker.

I cringe. "Jessa, no!"

"I'm not letting you go if you don't take someone with you, so who else? Maybe that policewoman? Maybe Lindy?"

A harsh point. But honestly, I've sort of gotten used to having someone in the passenger seat, and if nothing else I could use a navigator. So after I shower and scrape my hair into a neat ponytail and, at the last moment, stuff a Ziploc bag of Lucky Charms into my coat pocket, I drive over to the Prices' house. A miserable-looking Jessa waves at me from their bay window while Chad slides into the frost-fogged car. Slumping down in his jacket with the ski pass permanently affixed to the zipper, he palms back the white-blond jumble of his hair and yawns, rubs his eyes with the heel of one hand. "Cold one, huh?"

So now we're talking about the weather. I fiddle with the heating vents to delay conversation. Like the coffee Lindy left in the pot Thursday night—bitter to begin with and by Friday morning, toxic—the awkwardness between us is exponentially worse in the daylight. I only make it halfway down Cedar before pulling onto a dead-end side street and throwing the Civic into park. "We know you know something's going on."

Carefully, Chad watches a pack of boys in winter jackets and athletic shorts wrestle for a basketball below a hoop at the end of the cul-de-sac. "It's your secret, Imogene. I'm sorry Jessa opened her mouth. You really don't need to tell me."

Untrue. I have to give him something if I want him to look at me the way he used to, and not as a doctor-in-training trying to diagnose the wounded. I breathe deeply. "We've been trying to find my dad. But I think—I know—Dad is looking for my mother. My real mom, I mean, who left when I was two years old. So, I am too. It's . . . complicated."

"Sounds like it." He whistles low. "That's heavy stuff."

"But thanks to you, we've kind of got a lead. Dr. Sorbousek told us that my mother said she was going back home, and we know she's from Fitchburg originally, so—"

"So that's where we're headed. Makes sense. But . . . are you okay?"

There's that question again. "Always," I quote my dad with a smile, hoping I sound so much cooler than I feel. Then Chad looks at me, studies me with perfect, sea-glass-green eyes and for a heart-pumping second I'm carried away by butterflies—no, bigger. By full-size Victoria crowned pigeons.

"You're so tough, Imogene Scott." He not-quite-smiles back. "How did you get to be so tough?"

Later, I'll come up with a thousand possible retorts. For now, I can only shrug and stare helplessly back until he flashes a dimple and shakes his head.

"So what's the plan when we get there?"

I perk up—my own strategic genius is a safer topic— and drop the envelope of bills Lindy left for me in his lap. Two hundred bucks! Seems like way too much money for a prom dress, but I'm not complaining. Fitchburg's more than an hour northwest, and my car is running on fumes and hope.

He flips through the cash, then sits up straighter. "Holy bankroll. Are we opening a meth lab?"

"We're 'buying a prom dress,'" I air-quote.

"Oh, well, now I understand why Jessa thought I should come along."

I throw the car into drive, and once we're moving forward again, I *feel* tough. Which is exactly what I want to be. Tough means strong. It means even if you're sad—or god forbid, lonely—you won't crumble like a dry granola bar in the bottom of a backpack, destined to spill out over the lap of the first person who fumbles open your foil wrapper. Tough is the opposite of troubled waters.

Calvinistic Congregational is beautiful. Old, ornate, and red-bricked, with a roof the light green color of weather-beaten copper, like the Statue of Liberty. It's the only building in Fitchburg I could find that matches the one in the photo of Lil and my mom. Chad and I stand on the sidewalk outside and tilt our heads back to examine the steepled clock towers from below.

"That's a *church*," Chad says.

"I agree." I turn in circles on the concrete. Behind us is Main Street, and beyond that is the Fitchburg Art Museum, which Wikipedia called "one of the most treasured cultural institutions in Central New England." A pretty high bar, considering the gallery of crayon-colored kids' placemats above the register at Bingo's Breakfast in Sugarbrook.

All around the church are businesses, some in old-style brick and brownstone, some in new but not particularly shiny white buildings. There's something labeled a "Theater Guild," a thrift store called Odds-N-Ends, a credit union, restaurants. According to Google Maps, the nearest homes lie directly northwest. But we don't walk straight there.

Shoving our hands into our pockets against the cold—the semi-warmth of last Wednesday at Victory Island has yet to be repeated—we plod a little ways down Circle Street, which crosses over a thin river, and there in front of us lies Crocker Field. The park where my mom and Lil used to stop on their way home from church. It's huge, ringed by a track and circled by tall trees, with painted lines for all kinds of sports. Probably it's gotten fancier since Mom was a kid.

"Did you ever play here?" I ask Chad.

"A couple of times in Fitchburg, yeah, but not in this park. Weren't you at one of the games? When Fitchburg's midfielder got hurt?"

That's right, I was. I used to tag along with the Prices to games, because why wouldn't I watch Chad's thighs sprint across a soccer field in nylon shorts? But the game Chad's talking about happened when he was a junior, and he collided with a boy in the center of the field. They went down together with a terrible dry sound I swear you could hear from the bleachers, like the husk being ripped from a corncob. Nobody knew whose body had broken until Chad untangled himself and bounced away, flushed and shaking but fine. The other boy wasn't; he'd shredded his knee. After that I got this sick, nervous feeling I couldn't control whenever I went to one of Chad's matches.

"Huh, I don't remember that." I shrug and we keep going, all the way around the field, onto Broad Street and then River Street, which spits us back onto Main a ways up from the church.

"Maybe we should go get the car and drive around for a while?" Chad suggests.

I chew the inside of my lip until I realize it's Jessa's nervous habit. "The house has to be close. My mom . . . she could hear the baseball games from the backyard. It must be one of these streets."

We cut across light traffic on Main Street and head up Chestnut, the first residential street nearest the field, comparing the houses on either side of the road to the photo clutched in my fingers. Their matted brown lawns peek through a dusting of snow that came in the night. Christmas lights still cling to one or two gutters. But I don't see the house, and Chestnut dead-ends after a block and a half. We backtrack to the cross street, Arlington, and head left in the direction of the field. That takes us to Prospect, where the houses seem entirely too big, thinning out into businesses just a little down the road.

Maybe this won't work after all. Maybe I won't recognize the house, or Lil was totally exaggerating when she said she could practically smell the ballpark hot dogs. I pry my phone out of my pocket and try her number again; no answer, and because I was too preoccupied with research to charge it last night, my phone is blinking on its last battery bar. So we're on our own for now.

There's a whole web of residential streets here spinning through the trees. On Google Maps it looked totally doable. On the ground, it's a different story. And what do I expect to find, anyway? Whether the stone in my satchel's front pocket is my grandmother's heart or not, she's dead for certain. Lil said Mom's father was gone too. And even if Mom did come home, what was left in her childhood house to come back to? Who knows if the people living there can even help me?

Still. I have to start somewhere. And even though Fitchburg is bigger than Sugarbrook, it's an old town and this is an old neighborhood, and just like in Sugarbrook, neighborhoods love to talk. And if there's one thing they like to talk about best, it's their sons and daughters. Where they are now. What they're doing. Who's moved to the big city and become a smash success. Who's been arrested and who got married and who came out of the closet and who died, and all the terrible things that happen to them along the way.

We head in the opposite direction. A few blocks past a cross street, it seems like we're getting too far from the field, so we turn around and head down Bond, where, three houses in on the left, I grab Chad's swishy ski jacket. My heart hammers against my ribs.

The little house isn't white—it's sort of a bluish purple, not even recently painted, and there's no flag hanging from the lamppost. But it has the same perfectly square windows, the chimney is in the right place, and though the tree in the yard is taller, it's definitely the forked white birch from the picture. I hold the photo up to be sure.

Chad double-checks the picture and smiles. "I think we found it."

I tuck the photo in my jacket pocket and try to crack my knuckles, before remembering I'm wearing puffy gloves. "I guess we should ring the doorbell."

He peels off his left glove, pulls my right glove off by the tips, and threads his fingers through mine. I don't even get to soak in the warmth of his skin, his callused palm, before my traitorous hand jerks away of its own free will. It's out of my control, like a sneeze.

I can feel my cold cheeks warm, embarrassed. "I didn't mean that. I don't . . . Sorry."

He nods. "Come on, tough guy."

Why? Why is this the moment my imperfect but generally reliable brain misfires?

Whatever the reason, I don't have time to think about it because we're moving: up the flagstone walk, up the steps to the miniature porch, toward the door with a little stained-glass bumblebee sticky-cupped to the side window. I reach out my hand, now in control, if shaky, and ring the doorbell.

And realize there's probably no one home. Because it's ten thirty on a Tuesday, and we've come all this way for nothing, and really, what could these people have told me anyway, since all the Fayes are gone—

The door opens.

"Help you?" asks a man, eyeing us down the long wedge of his nose. Wearing only a Red Sox T-shirt and sweats over bare feet, he crosses his arms against the wind. Something tells me he's not a long-lost Faye.

I skim my tongue over my dry lips. "Yeah. Yes. Sorry to bother you, it's just, I'm doing a school project and I, um, wondered if you might have a minute to help me?"

"Aren't you guys on break from school?" Scattered in the hallway behind him, I notice kid-colored backpacks, and smallish sneakers with light-up bottoms.

"I know, it sucks, right?" Chad laughs. "Homework over vacation?"

I shrug in a *What are you going to do?* way.

"I don't know. I'm just off my night shift. About to head to bed. You're not selling magazines or anything, are you?"

"No way. And just a second is all I need," I say gratefully. "One point five seconds at most. See, we're supposed to do a report on our family history in the area. And my mom, she has this cousin I never met. Sidonie Faye? They haven't talked in a while, since Sidonie moved away, but Mom said she lived in this house growing up. And she thought Sidonie might've moved back into the area. I know it's a long shot, but I was just wondering if you knew her, if she might've come back here, in the past few years?"

"This is a school project?" He lifts a bristly black eyebrow.

"Yep. For social studies—applying big lessons to our little lives, you know? Oh, and I have a picture!" I dig into my bag, pulling out the brochure from the Boston MFA. I flip to the exhibit photo and spread it out for the guy. I notice Chad examining it slyly, then looking at me. For comparison?

The man in the Sox T-shirt shrugs. "Tell you the truth, we just moved in three years ago, and we didn't buy the house from a Faye. You know who you might ask? Tilly Donahue." He points to a squat brown house two properties down, its lawn potholed with grassless patches, plastic pinwheels poking up through the gnarly shrubs around the porch. "She's lived here some fifty years, got her nose in everybody's business. Let's say she knows when the mayor takes a squat."

"Uh-huh. So, she's usually home?"

"Right now, she's at . . . what do you call . . . water aerobics or something. For old people. Her home aid will bring her back around one thirty, after they do their shopping. I know this because she comes knocking every damn day at one forty-five to change a bulb or fix her doorbell or some nonsense. And I work nights, you know?"

"Right, yeah, I'll definitely check with her. Thanks for your time."

Chad nods his thanks, and we leave his porch as the door shuts tight, the bumblebee rattling in the window.

"So." He blows into his cupped hands.

We stand on the front walk under a tent of thick gray clouds, without anywhere in particular to go. It's not even eleven now. That's a lot of time to be alone with Chad Price.

"I guess we could sit somewhere, get coffee or something?" I offer. There must be a coffee place or two in Fitchburg. A Starbucks at least. With my petty cash, I can even afford to put whipped cream in mine.

Chad taps a finger against his chin. "Or we could find you a prom dress."

I stare at him.

"Isn't that your alibi?"

"It wasn't an alibi so much as a lie."

"So what'll you tell Lindy when you come home with no dress?"

"I'll—"

"And what will you do when prom comes? Tell her you're going, then run and hide in the attic?" He pokes my shoulder, though I can't really feel it through the down in my coat. "You've lied yourself into a corner, Imogene, and that is the corner of the Sugarbrook gymnasium on prom night. What do you think the theme will be? Ours was 'This Recession Has Really Killed Our Prom Budget.'"

I remember Chad's prom night. I saw it happening from the window in my living room, having elbowed aside the old plaid drapes. My fingers were chalked orange from the supersize tub of Cheez Doodles wedged between newlyweds Dad and Lindy on the sofa. They were settling in to watch *The Thin Man*. It was Dad's 111th viewing and Lindy's first. As the opening credits ran, I spied on Chad and his date, Beth Holmes, posing for pictures in the Prices' driveway. From a block away they were only specks, him black and white in his suit, her glittering in blue, a diamond that'd caught the sun. Beth was not only the girls' tennis team captain, she was president of Key Club, the collection of mostly popular girls who rang bells for the Salvation Army around the holidays, organized G-rated car washes for the local animal shelters in the spring, stuff like that. Though I couldn't see the details from that distance, I could imagine them. Her tennis arms, her petal-pink lipstick, her signature fruity perfume smell. And not cheap-fruity, like girls who bought spritzers in plastic spray bottles at

Walmart. Expensive, designer-fruity. Pomegranate with hints of saffron and ancient redwood, or something.

I watched their shiny, shell-white limo glide by, knowing Jessa and Jeremy were in there too, behind the black windows. Jessa was the only sophomore at prom that year, and in her gold dress and with her flat-ironed red-gold hair, she looked like a living Oscar statuette. She looked fantastic in every picture I saw of her afterward, and I saw so many.

When May rolls around she'll go with Jeremy again, I'm sure. I was planning on staying home and watching *Ace in the Hole* with Dad. Or maybe going for our traditional Spicy Italian on flatbread and Chicken and Bacon Ranch Melt in our booth by the door, for old time's sake.

But Chad's right. I have lied myself into a corner, unless the school gym burns down.

Could I burn the school gym down?

I could not.

I flail around for a reasonable excuse, landing on "If I spend all my cash on a prom dress, I won't have any money for gas. I'll be right back where I started."

He taps his chin again as he thinks. "So, get a cheap dress."

I give him the side-eye.

"Oh, come on. You could find something at Home

Depot and it'd look better on you than all the girls who shopped on Newbury."

"Untrue." To hide my blush, I fiddle with the strap on my bag. "And I don't think Home Depot sells prom dresses."

"There's a thrift store in town. Not thrift . . . consignment? We always stopped at the Olive Garden to eat after Fitchburg games, and there's a place next to it. It has tons of girlie dresses in the window. Little Mermaid–style and everything. Jessa said they were 'like, cute for secondhand.'"

"This doesn't seem like a productive use of our time." A Lindy-ism, if ever I've repeated one.

He shrugs. "It's your choice. But you're stuck, and you need to find something, unless you can weave a gown out of *lies*."

I'm hoping we won't find the store. Unfortunately, Chad has a fantastic memory. Once we backtrack to the Calvinistic Congregational parking lot and pick up my car, it doesn't take him long to find the Olive Garden and the thrift store—sorry, *consignment* shop—next to it. The bells above the door jingle as we slip into Suzanne's Dress for Less. A salesgirl waves at us and asks if we need any help, but I can't stop staring at the height of her fancy heels, like bamboo stilts.

I wade cautiously toward the rack of dresses along

the back wall, while Chad plunges in. He pulls one out and holds it up at arm's length. It's scaly and slightly iridescent, a kind of mystery fabric that flashes olive green and copper and gold at certain angles. "Reptilian," he comments. "Very cool."

I trail my fingertips across silk and sequins and a lot of Frankenstein-style polyester blends. There's a knee-length pink thing that looks like an iced cupcake, and a long yellow gown shaped like a partially peeled banana. I find a shimmering silver dress and start to pick it up, but when I think of the one Jessa lent me, crumpled at the bottom of my hamper and smelling of rum and misery, I sour on the idea and shove it back.

This is stupid. I'll think up an excuse before prom. Play sick, somehow. Or Dad will get me out of it. . . .

Uneasiness simmers in the pit of my stomach. I shouldn't be thinking of prom or pretty dresses or Chad, not when Dad's been away without a word for six days now. I try to check the time on my phone before discovering it's dead, then pull Chad's wrist up to read the digits on his big calculator watch. One hour before Tilly is back from Water Aerobics for the Ancient. An hour and I might have some answers. What's an hour? I've waited six days. I can wait sixty minutes. Besides, he's not missing, I remind myself. Just searching, like I am.

"How's this?"

Chad plucks out a dress and dangles it by the hanger. And it's . . . not terrible. Vintage-looking, but not old-fashioned. Deep red, like wine, with a heart-shape neckline, a high waist, and the kind of full, just-below-the-knee skirt Jessa claims works for sizable thighs. It's the kind of dress a girl might wear in the old noir mysteries Dad likes. In those movies, a girl is either good, or she's one of *those* girls, as Liz Bash would say. Either a Mrs. Maximilian de Winter, or a Rebecca. This is the kind of dress one of *those* girls might wear when she's still acting sweet in front of the detective, but we on our couches with our Cheez Doodles know she's trouble.

It's a pretty sexy dress. A pretty sexy dress that Chad is holding out to me with one eyebrow raised, and a smile I've never quite seen before.

As I stand here considering it, I ask myself, what do I know?

I know I've had this Guinness Book of World Records Longest-Running Crush on Chad since fifth grade. I remember the exact night it happened. A girl in Jessa's ballet class had told her how to summon Bloody Mary, and she wanted to play the game. Even kid-size Jessa was pretty good at getting what she wanted. While she chanted the name three times in the flickering light of a Glade candle, I stayed by the bathroom door, knowing that just outside, Chad had sweetly volunteered to stand guard. Just in case Mary showed, he said. When he rattled the knob violently I screamed, tripped over a wet towel that might've been Mary's grasping, bloodied arm on the dark bathroom floor, and burst out into Chad's arms, Jessa close behind. Tucked into his then-scrawny chest, he smelled like mint and strange spices at once (toothpaste and boy deodorant, I later realized). That was it. The die was cast.

I have never asked a guy out in my life. Haven't even slipped one a "Do you like me? Circle yes or no" note. Lee Jung asked me to be his girlfriend, and Jeff Keating asked to kiss me behind the bounce house at the low-budget Sugarbrook fair that goes up in the mall parking lot each year, and A.J. Breen, the only boy to write me love letters, slipped a cartoon drawing of me drinking a milkshake into my Trapper Keeper in middle school, asking me to sit with him at lunch. But I never asked anything from a guy. What's the upside? The possible outcomes as I see it are:

1) I'll like them but they won't like me, resulting in pain.

2) We'll go out and I'll realize I don't like them and have to dump them, resulting in pain.

3) We'll go out and I'll end up really liking the boy, only to have him dump me for Cassie Pavia, who stands at the electronic pencil sharpener in front of Josh Davis's

desk with her hip popped while Josh moans, "Cassie, you're *killing* me with that body." Result: Pain.

I mean, how are two people ever supposed to like each other the right amount in the right way at the right time? Impossible.

But I also know that Chad Price is looking at me with big green eyes and one dimpled cheek, his blond hair fuzzed from pawing through racks of fabric, all of this making me warm and misty, and he's offering me a beautiful dress that I want him to see me in. Are these random occurrences, or fate? Unconnected dots or a constellation? And isn't this what I'm supposed to be doing?

Having faith?

For once, don't be tough, I tell myself. Be brave.

I snatch the hanger away. "I will try this on if, *if . . .*"

"If?"

I inspect the crisp red fabric, the size (seems right), the fifty-five-dollar price tag (about forty more than I wanted to spend), the stitching along the neckline (like he believes I'm fascinated by the construction of this dress). "If you put on a suit and come to prom too."

His smile wobbles, confused.

"Just, if I have to go, I don't see why you get off. You're my accomplice in this." I stare at the dress in his arms and wonder if he can sense the breath trapped in my body.

"I can see I've been tangled in your web of lies," he says, grinning again. "Yeah, I'll go."

I sweep off to the fitting rooms, keeping it together pretty well. But as I kick my boots and jeans off and slide into the gown, the fist of my heart unclenches, and maybe it's the blood flowing again, the air pumping in and out of my lungs (so much air, I can't get enough of it! And it all smells wonderful!), and I know I shouldn't, but I feel so light. I'm a mayfly on the breeze. A balloon. A beam of moonlight. A sun.

FOURTEEN

While we wait in my car for Tilly Donahue's return from elderly water aerobics, the sky spits freezing rain that blurs the windshield. The last real clumps of snow beside the storm drains glitter dangerously; fresh ice will make for a thrilling drive home. But it's dry in the Civic, the heater sputtering heroically onward, and Chad and I are playing the picnic game.

"I'm going to a picnic and I'm bringing an apple, a barracuda, Captain Morgan, a deciduous pine, elephantiasis of the balls, a falafel truck, and . . . Gaussian frequency-shift keying." He smiles, triumphant, little

C's punctuating the corners of his lips.

"I bet you don't even know what that is."

"That is not a requirement in the picnic game." He grabs a fistful of Lucky Charms from my Baggie, which we've been passing back and forth, and separates out the marshmallows. Sorts them further in piles of balloons, horseshoes, rainbows. They all taste like sweet packing peanuts to me, but I like that he bothers. He dusts the cereal bits from his palm into my waiting hand, and his eyes light up. "And I do *so* know what Gaussian frequency-shift keying is, because we're doing a unit of FSK modulation in my engineering elective. It uses a Gaussian filter to—"

"Fine." I dump the cereal in my mouth and sneak a look in the rearview mirror. My dress hangs in its black plastic garment bag in the backseat, like a promise. "I'm going to a picnic and I'm bringing an apple, a barracuda, Captain Morgan, a deciduous pine, elephantiasis of the balls, a falafel truck, Gaussian frequency-shift keying, and Hannah Montana."

Chad's lip curls. "Of all the picnics in the world, this is the worst. You couldn't bring Hillary Clinton?"

"Take your Captain Morgan and your elephantiasis of the balls and go, or keep playing."

"No, let's play a different game. Let's play I Spy."

"I hate that game," I protest.

"Nobody hates I Spy."

"I do. Oh, 'I spy something gray.' But it's February in New England. It's all gray."

"Okay." He tosses a marshmallow heart in the air and catches it with a click of his jaws. "What about Would You Rather?"

I know this is his way of distracting me, but better a stupid game than sitting in a silent car, cracking my knuckles until they ache and feeling more nervous by the second. "Okay. Would you rather be able to read books, or be able to read minds?"

"I can't read books if I can read minds?"

"One or the other."

He drums two fingers against his lips, and I remember my fixation on his mouth in his basement bedroom. "Reading minds would make it easier to be a doctor. But let's say books. I'm pretty sure the majority of minds are boring. At least in Sugarbrook they are. Present company excluded."

A good answer. "Would you rather . . ."

"You already had your turn, turn-taker. Now it's mine." He roots around in the Baggie for a last marshmallow bit and comes out empty. "Would you rather . . . be able to go to the future, or be able to visit the past?"

"Are we talking my past, or the past of humanity?"

"Your past. Not, like, Oregon-Trail-and-long-underwear past."

"Easy. The past." The rain's falling a little heavier now. I watch it blacken Tillys' driveway in inky splatters.

"Why? What if the future's awesome?"

"With global warming? Unlikely. And I like the past. It was nice. All our problems were easier."

It's true. I mean, it wasn't all lollipops and Disney movies, but the past is safe. If I could visit, I'd find all the happy parts with Dad and me and live in them over and over. And besides, I honestly don't know what I want from my future anymore, because at this moment I have no idea what it will look like. If Tilly Donahue is the lead that helps me find my mom and dad . . . then what? I'm not wishing on a star for my biological parents to get back together, get married, book us all on a big family road trip. I know my mom's got real problems. So I don't believe that this time tomorrow we'll be outfitting the guest room in Mom's favorite color (blue, like Dad's? Red, like mine?). I don't know what the world will look like with all of us in it. But it has to be so much better than not knowing her.

Chad nods. "Yeah. I kind of miss my old problems too. When losing your science textbook under your bed was this huge deal. And I could tell my mom I wanted to be a doctor without having to worry about actually being a doctor, or getting into the right programs, or the right hospital, or being happy."

"But you want to be a doctor, don't you?"

He gives a helpless little half laugh. "I'd better."

"Hmm. So what would you pick? The past or the future?"

When he looks at me and bites his lip, I feel my pulse in my ears, and I think this is what it feels like to really want a boy.

Whether he would've picked the past or the future, I'll never find out, because a beige car pulls up the driveway of the little brown house. Tilly Donahue and her home aide, I presume. The aide slides out, waddles to the other side of the car, and gently pries the old woman out by the elbow. She guides her across the icy-slick flagstones along the front walk. All I can see of Tilly is a cloud of permed white hair above the collar of her fur coat. Who wears a fur coat to water aerobics?

Quickly they duck inside, out of the weather.

"Ready?" Chad asks.

"Yeah," I whisper, then louder, "yes."

When we're shivering and blinking frozen water out of our eyes on the sidewalk, he offers me his hand. "In case I slip," he says, and smiles.

I take it this time and even though I'm out of the

beautiful red dress that made all my weird curves look like they were supposed to be there, back in my hoodie with the chewed drawstrings and jeans with Swiss-cheese knees, I could almost dance up the driveway and onto the porch. I ring the doorbell, and with his free hand Chad palms back his hair, wet and peaked with rain.

The narrow young face of the home aide floats in the window. "Hello?" She answers the door, still hung with a glittery Valentine's Day wreath of pink hearts speared with arrows. Without her own coat on, I can see she's hugely pregnant under a tent of a sweater.

"Hi!" I chirp, and repeat the story of the school project, the long-lost aunt. I'm getting pretty slick at lying my way into people's homes. Which I don't think is wrong. Maybe just . . . Machiavellian. "So Tilly's neighbor said she might be the best person to help us. Since she knows a lot of what happens in town."

The aide laughs. "He's not wrong. Just hold on while I ask Tilly? She might be tired out."

Ten minutes later and with glasses of lime seltzer in our hands and a bowl of licorice hard candies in front of us, Chad and I are sitting down on the couch in Tilly's living room. There's a definite theme going on—framed embroideries of shamrocks and saints and those little hand-heart-crown combos all over. On the shelf above the fireplace are dozens of little ceramic leprechauns. In an armchair under a big stained-glass wall hanging of the green, white, and orange Irish flag sits Tilly Donahue: a hawk-nosed, coral-lipped, bird-boned woman in a caramel velour tracksuit. There are a dozen rings at least on her bent fingers, big, polished hunks of pink and blue and green and tiger-eye stone. As she fiddles with the cellophane wrapper on licorice after licorice, she's only too happy to talk. She's already complained to us about the weather, her sore hip, her nasal congestion, and her cataracts with the same pride in her cloudy eyes as a collector showing off her prized postage stamps. The aide retreated to the kitchen after settling Tilly in. Probably she's heard all of this three times today already.

When I tell Tilly I'm looking for one of the Fayes—"the Protestants down the street," she calls them—she really gets revved up.

"The mother, she ran off early. When the girl was, oh, eight or nine. Siobhan was a strange fruit. And that poor Sidonie, she never had much chance at normal. Do you know she used to knock on my door and ask for things like milk? Because her father used to forget to buy it. Imagine, a little girl in the house and you don't buy milk. And the milkman hadn't been coming around for fifteen years! The father always offered to shovel my driveway after a big one, before he was taken and they shipped the girl across town. But he went away on business a lot, and anyway, a little girl needs a mother. Or else they don't learn how to act. I think it must be why all these girls on TV are going to jail and showing around their privates. They show their privates in the streets like parade floats!"

Chad splutters around a sip of seltzer. I have zero percent desire to hear Tilly Donahue's theories on why motherless girls like me grow up to show around their privates, but she seems to be waiting for my answer. For something to do, I peel the wrapper off a licorice and pop it into my mouth. It tastes like the bottom of a 1950s-style candy man's pocket. "Huh," I gargle, tucking the sugary rock into my cheek. "So, do you know what happened to Sidonie when she grew up? My mom . . . Lil . . . she thought her cousin might've come back to Fitchburg about five years ago."

"She did." Tilly bobs her head on her thin neck, and this seed of excitement sprouts in me. "And that was something. Twenty years, the Faye girl disappears. No one knows where she went, then one day Margie Goldberg says she saw her in the Stop and Shop with Todd Malachai." She lowers her voice and leans in. "And one week Todd came in and bought ladies' unmentionables."

"Uh-huh . . ."

"The Malachais used to live over on River Street. I

think Sidonie and Todd were little school friends. And they went to church together. They were Protestants, too, you know."

The candy is a sharp-edged, sickly sweet disk between my teeth. "So Sidonie's here now? Staying with Todd?"

"I didn't say that," she answers, clearly having a fantastic time. "You know Margie's son-in-law is a janitor at New Hope, and he says Todd dropped Sidonie off for all her appointments. And Todd was living over by the bowling alley then, so that was all the way across town."

"What's New Hope?" Chad asks for me.

"The Thorndyke Center for New Hope is the whole name. There was a vote in the town hall, when they wanted to put it up, and it nearly didn't pass because no one wanted . . . We were all just worried what kind of people it might attract into town. Do you know I've lived here since I was born? Not in this house the whole time; I grew up in the part of town they called Tar Hill. Now they put up New Hope over there, so who knows what's become of it?" She leans forward again, presses her thin orange-pink lips together. "It's a place for the mentally *unfirm.*"

I can't get the words "troubled waters" out of my head. "It's a mental hospital?"

"I don't know what you call it. More like . . ." Her old forehead crinkles in thought. "What are those places, where the drunks meet up to talk about being drunks?"

"Um . . . Alcoholics Anonymous?"

"Yes. But for the unfirm. That's how they explained it to us at town hall, anyway."

I don't really know what any of this means, but Tilly plows right on through.

"Margie—she's the one of them that works at Stop and Shop ever since she mostly retired—she says Todd used to pick up her prescriptions for her, sometimes. For Sidonie, I mean." She lets out a hoarse clap of laughter. "That's really something, isn't it? Do you know, those two went to their high school prom together?"

So Todd is the tall boy standing behind Mom in his big-shouldered suit. I guess he really was thrilled to be with her. "Do they still live by that bowling alley?"

"Oh, no." Tilly leans back, working at another candy wrapper. I just want to smack it out of her grip, and maybe Chad senses this, because he squeezes my hand in his. With a little squawk of victory, she fishes out the licorice and pops it in her mouth. "He moved away about two years ago. Hilda Malachai—that's his great-aunt—says he works at a college in Connecticut now. What's the big one?"

"UConn?" Chad offers.

"Yes, that's it, I want to say. Not a teacher, though." She sniffs. "Something in the office."

"Did my mom's cousin . . . Did she go with him when he left town?"

"I don't know. I wouldn't guess so. Might be Hilda could tell you, though I don't think she'll be much help. She's not altogether *firm* herself. Touch of the dementia, poor thing. Mostly we see each other over at the church. She's there an awful lot. Her home aide brings her over. I go every Sunday, myself. Who sins enough to go every day?"

"Do you know how we can get in touch with her?" I ask. A lead is a lead.

"I don't think I should give her number out. You never know what people can do with that information, everything you hear on the news about identity theft."

Chad and I exchange side eyes; do I seem likely to steal the identity of a senile, serial church-goer? "Oh, that's too bad. I'd really love to talk to your friend."

"I suppose *I* can call her up." Tilly's smile sharpens, thrilled to play a part in the little drama unfolding before her.

When Hilda answers, Tilly catches her up (at top volume and with much repetition) about me and my mission to find my "aunt." Then she hands me the receiver of her clunky corded phone, keeping a finger curled in the wire. I speak to Hilda on a short leash.

"Hi, Mrs. Malachai. I really appreciate your taking the time to—"

"Hello?"

"Um, hi?"

Across from me, Chad winces. We're off to a rocky start.

"Tilly said you have questions for me," Hilda's sandpaper voice rasps across the receiver, "about one of Todd's old girlfriends?"

"Sidonie Faye. Yes, your friend says she used to live with Todd? Above the bowling alley?"

"Oh, I don't know. That's asking a lot of me."

Her head cocked toward the receiver to hear, Tilly nods, looking a little victorious to be proven right.

"He's very handsome, like his grandfather Jacob," Hilda continues. "My brother had so many sweethearts when he was young. So did Todd. He always had another little girlfriend to bring around the holidays."

"This one would've been just two or three years ago. Um, she had brown hair and hazel eyes. She was small. And . . . I guess she might've been a little sick at the time. Or just . . . troubled?"

It's not much, as vital statistics go, but Hilda surprises me by answering, "There *was* one girl he went around with. *She* was trouble. Made his father so upset, it broke his heart. She was a pretty little white girl, but she was crazier than a sack of raccoons, would borrow money from Todd because she didn't work. Crashed this truck he had at the time. All kinds of problems. But I thought that was a while back. My nephew passed when that second Bush was still president. Or was that my cousin's son? Oh, there's too many of them to keep track."

So Hilda's not the most reliable source. But I don't want her sketchy memory for details to distract me from the big picture. "Do you think it's possible Todd kept in touch with her?"

"Well, I don't know why he would. His mother says he's married now, to a lovely woman in New York. But who knows? He doesn't come home much. Doesn't report in to me. I don't even have his number."

"You mean Connecticut?"

"What's that?"

"He's in Connecticut, not New York. Right? I thought he worked at UConn."

"Sure, maybe he does."

"All right, that's . . . helpful. Thanks."

Having heard the whole conversation, Tilly sips her seltzer primly and says when I've hung up, "You know, ever since Siobhan went off the rails, I knew her little girl was headed for a hard time."

We can't get out of there fast enough.

We head back to Sugarbrook as the sky really opens up and icy raindrops the size of pebbles pelt the car roof. We drive in silence, deafened. But I'm not sulking. We're closing in on Sidonie Faye. When Dad and I find her, it won't matter that she quit a few jobs and crashed her ex-boyfriend's truck and went a little off the rails. She'll have her family to help her out. Besides, I knew she was troubled waters from the start. This was never going to be easy.

Without thinking, I smile over at Chad. "Want to help us track down Todd Malachai?"

"That's the spirit!" he says, and shakes me gently by the neck the way he does when we play video games. His hand is big and dry and warm.

When we're almost home we drive ahead of the weather, and the clouds turn white all at once and the last bit of sun streaks through. I think there must be a rainbow somewhere, with the road still glittering. While we're stopped at a light I crane my neck around to search the gray block of sky behind me, but there's nothing there.

FIFTEEN

"You're spending quite a lot of time with them." Lindy works to free the zipper where it's caught on the black plastic. "I don't want you getting in their hair . . . Oh, Immy!" She gasps. Red fabric tumbles out of the bag. "You're going to look so beautiful! Did you try it on? Do you love it?"

Is it my imagination, or are my stepmother's cool blue eyes a little dewy? "I guess. It's no big deal or anything."

"It is a big deal," she corrects me. "I just can't believe how mature you are. You're almost a grown-up."

I don't like the "almost" part—I'm the grown-up who's hot on my dad's trail. Not Lindy, not Officer Griffin, not anybody older or supposedly more mature than me. But it doesn't help my case to argue the compliment. "Thanks, Lindy."

Running her fingers over the skirt of the dress, the slightly plunging neckline, and the thick red halter straps, she sighs. "I want you to know how proud I am of you, Immy. Of how you're handling yourself in all of this. And I know your dad . . ." She covers her mouth with a shaking hand and coughs out an ugly half sob.

It's totally horrifying. I have no idea what to do, what to say. I get awkward around tears, embarrassed; for the crier or for myself as the cried-upon, I don't know. Probably both. I almost always knew how to handle Dad in his bad times. I could lead him to bed when he'd drunk too much on a very not-great night, make myself breakfast the next morning, get myself to the school bus and leave a list of things for him to do that day, because sometimes he needed a reason to climb out of bed. I'm well-equipped for that. But crying? Usually I would fall back on a bad joke: *Hey, Dad, two cows were standing in a field. The first said, 'What do you think about this mad cow disease?' The second said, 'Doesn't bother me, I'm a duck.' Get it? Because he's crazy? Come on, Dad, that's funny.*

I can't think of a joke to tell Lindy, and the moment drags on. And on.

"I'm sorry, Immy." She thumbs a tear from the corner of her eye. "Don't pay attention to me. I'm just . . . This is a beautiful dress. Maybe we can find an updo to match—something old-fashioned and romantic?"

"Yeah." I smile for her. "Maybe."

"I'll hang this up in the hall closet, okay? I don't think there's much space in yours, and I don't want it to wrinkle."

When she whisks the garment bag out of the room, I seize my chance and back toward the front door. My hand on the knob, I call, "Lindy, I'll be back after dinner, okay? Not too late! And then maybe we can talk about . . . prom shoes!" Then I'm out and away and free and gulping big, grateful breaths of freezing air, like a fish thrown back into the sea after finding itself caught in a net.

Though I was only making an excuse to investigate Todd Malachai with Jessa and Chad, it turns out the Prices really are making dinner when they let me in out of the rain. They invite me to eat with them, so I can't exactly refuse. On a normal day I love eating with Jessa's family, which is thoroughly normal and one I admit I've sometimes pretended was my own. Tonight, it's all I can do to joke with them in the kitchen when I've got my freshest lead yet, waiting to be chased. For a minute I consider begging off, going back home, locking myself in my bedroom to try to find Todd myself. But I've gotten used to having partners these past few days. It didn't even occur to me to look him up alone, and how weird is that?

"Up high, Immy." Mr. Price holds his hand in prime high-five position, and though Jessa rolls her eyes, I slap his palm. He has the same white-blond hair as Chad, though he doesn't have his son's tan or sweet green eyes or flat stomach or awesome sense of humor. He's just spectacularly, typically father-like. I can smell his familiar cologne over the tuna sizzling on their stovetop grill.

"How was your business trip?" I ask.

He scratches his neat beard. "France was enriching, as always."

"It's France." Jessa cuts between us to dump a stack of modern-looking square bowls on the table. "It smells like old cheese."

Swiveling on a barstool at the kitchen island, Chad snorts. "Really? That's all you got out of France?"

"Yes, Chadwick. And the memory of the seagull that shit on you under the Arc de Triomphe. That was, like, such a Kodak moment."

Dr. Van Tassel, looking spa-fresh, raps her spatula on the stove twice as a warning, but Chad slow-claps.

"Oh, wow, *Jenessa.* Your worldly expertise is so wasted in Sugarbrook. You should go someplace where they'll truly appreciate your international experience. Some kind of house of pancakes, maybe?"

Jessa starts to give him the finger, but sheathes it when Dr. Van Tassel barks, "Knock it off, or eat in the driveway!"

Mr. Price washes a lettuce head at the sink, unconcerned. And me, I stay out of the way in the corner, steal glances at their reflections in the stainless-steel counters and fridge and toasting/microwaving/can-opening/bottle-opening/popcorn-popping appliances, all polished into mirrors. From every angle, they look perfect. I watch them and try to imagine Dad and me and Sidonie Faye . . . and Lindy . . . crammed into our kitchen at 42 Cedar Lane, with its dark, dull cabinets, its banana magnets, our flour and sugar begrudgingly spilled into canisters. But I can't picture my mom at the kitchen table, folding a napkin in her lap, buttering a roll. It's too . . . normal.

I'm too anxious to eat much, but I sit with them for dinner: grilled tuna, garlic biscuits from Jeanne's Cakes and Bakes (the only decent bakery in town since Jamison's closed), and bowls of cold edamame. We teethe the beans from their pods and chuck the deflated green skins in our little square bowls. Chad and Jessa fight happily over the third-to-last and then second-to-last and then the last biscuit on the platter. Dr. Van Tassel continues to be super-size-nice, which means she knows that Dad continues to be absent, but it doesn't bother me the way it once did. Mr. Price talks about the challenges of selling lighting equipment to other companies, which is the business he's in, coincidentally.

When I've nervously ground my tuna into pink confetti and the food is mostly gone, we excuse ourselves from the table. Chad stays behind to throw everything into the dishwasher, flicking detergent water at his sister. He pauses to brush away a stray sud that catches in my hair before Jessa and I retreat up the stairs. "So you and Chadwick seem friendly, no? Had a good time in Fitchburg, did you?" she says.

I can't help the smile that spreads across my face. "Friendly in the sense of friends, or friendly in the sense of prom dates?"

"Wait, what?" she shrieks, and wraps her fingers around my wrist and drags me into the bathroom of Bloody Mary to talk in secret, which seems unnecessary, since there's ten feet of hallway between us and her bedroom at most. "How did this happen? When did this happen? You're going to be my prom sister-in-law!"

"Okay, calm down." I bite back another smile.

"*Ugh,*" Jessa groans. "Can you not humor me and

girl out for, like, one single second?"

"Maybe after the call," I lie. Though a big part of me wants to squeal like a six-year-old girl at a birthday party, I've had a very successful run of not letting Jessa get too worked up. Dad has highs and lows, so I like to keep to an even-keeled middle. The same principle helps me to tether Jessa.

But it's hard not to get excited when finally, something comes easy. Jessa has the White Pages app on her iPhone, and there's only one Todd Malachai in eastern Connecticut, in a town called Windham. I write all of the info in his listing on my palm with Jessa's gold glitter Sharpie so I can enter it in my phone when I finally get around to charging it. I'll put in Lil's as well, and maybe Tilly's (though probably not Tilly's), which will bring my contacts up to a whopping fifteen or so.

Chad joins us as I'm rehearsing my now-familiar script about the school project. Because Jessa's texting—probably Jeremy—Chad generously donates his phone to the cause.

I tell myself not to get carried away. According to Hilda Malachai, my mom spun out pretty hard. Why Todd would keep in touch with the girl he drove to therapy and bought unmentionables for, only to have her leech his money and crash his truck, I don't know. Especially if he's married now. But maybe he can give me the clue that leads me to the clue that takes me to my parents. Anything is possible. And there's still New Hope. If this turns out to be a dead end, I can try them afterward. They might have records left from when my mom was there, and since it was only a few years ago, I might not even have to go digging through some dusty basement to find them.

First things first: make the call.

I press the phone against my cheek and wait while it rings. Next to me, Jessa twists her long hair between her hands, strangling it into golden knots I know she'll regret later. Chad plops down into the lips chair, digging his sister's old Cabbage Patch doll out from underneath him. He holds the arms out and folds the cloth fingers down so it's giving me a thumbs-up.

A woman answers on the fourth ring. "Hello?"

I stutter, unprepared for a female voice. "Um, hi. Um, is . . . is Todd there?"

"He's not home right now," she says. "Can I have him call you back?"

"Is this his wife?"

"It is," she says brightly.

I sigh internally. "Oh, sure. Just, if he could give me a call at some point tonight." I give my number, intending to plug my phone in as soon as I get home.

There's silence on the other end, and then, "Would

that be a Sugarbrook number?" The voice is smaller now, further away.

An uncomfortable numbness starts in the back of my neck and seeps outward, into my cheeks, toward my lips. I realize I'm breathing fast. "You're Mrs. Malachai?"

"Who is this?"

The tingling is spreading down my arms. "Not . . . not Sidonie Malachai."

The woman clears her throat. "Yes."

"No, but—" My fingertips are numb now, bloodlessly white around the phone.

"And who are you?"

I jab at the screen until I hit something that ends the call, then stare at the phone.

"What—"

"Jessa," Chad cuts her off quietly. The room is so quiet, in fact, that when his phone frog-croaks in my hand, we all jump. "It's a text," he says, blushing.

For one crazy, panicked moment I think it must be from my mother and I punch my finger into the text bubble. It reads: *Hi, you. Long day at the slopes, and sooo tired after last night. It was worth it. ;) Can't wait to see you again!* My eyes flick to the name above the message.

"It's Pari," I say dully, tossing Chad his phone.

He catches it easily and reads her text, and though he very considerately wipes the smile from his face almost instantly, his eyes brighten. He likes Pari and her winky-face and he likes whatever they did last night, which was tiring but worth it.

How stupid am I to think he agreed to go to prom as anything but a pity date for his little sister's friend? Of course that's the truth. He's a nice guy, and I am pitiful. This whole mission to find my dad by finding my mom was pitiful. Because my mother is not troubled waters. She is not lost. She is not holed up with Dad in some secretive place while he tries to save her for the both of us, which I believed since I discovered the heart in my nightstand.

My mother is married. My mother lives in Windham. My mother has a new last name, and my dad is nowhere.

"I'm gonna go," I manage. "Gotta charge my phone." Without another glance at Chad in the lips chair, I grab my stuff and hurry out of the room.

Jessa follows me into the hall. "Wait, Im, was that really your—"

"Uh-huh," I mumble, slipping into my coat and zipping it to the neck. If I'm this cold already, I might just freeze to death before I reach home.

"Well, that's awesome!"

I turn on her. "What are you talking about?"

Jessa beams. "Im, you just talked to your mother for, like, the first time ever. You really did it, you found her! We thought she was a wreck or something, but it sounds like she's fine. Isn't that a good thing? Maybe now she can help us out with your dad."

I study my friend, so cool in her skinny jeans and hot-pink one-shouldered sweater, her nails newly French manicured. My beautiful, perfect friend, with her beautiful, perfect body, surrounded by her beautiful, perfect family, in her beautiful, perfect home. While eighth-grade me was teaching myself to cook mac 'n' cheese and trying to convince my father he couldn't live off clove cigarettes and PBR and three a.m. infomercials, the Prices were "fine." And god, they always will be.

I cross my legs to hide the ragged hole in the knee of my jeans. "Just do me a favor. Fuck off."

Jessa's lips part, then press together. "I'm trying to help you. So is Chad."

"Like he wanted to help me out with prom? Yeah, no thanks. You shouldn't have even told Chad, or your asshole boyfriend. That was unbelievably stupid."

"First, we're not even going out." Jessa's blue eyes ice over as she tilts her head sharply to the side. "And you're saying I'm stupid?"

It's too late to go back now—all my misery is boiling

into this sick, hot rage that makes me want to tear down the plaster walls, smash the picture frames, shatter the chrome vases on their little tables—crash, kick, destroy, ruin. Why did I think this girl could help me? Jessa has never had to search for anyone or anything, ever. She's never had to worry, or hope, or wonder. Any mysteries in Jessa's life have been solved as easily as finding her missing lip gloss in the bottom of her fourth-favorite purse. I let this feeling fill me up, and it's so much better than feeling pathetic. I shrug. "Should I say it slower?"

"You know what? Whatever." Her face is almost calm except for one dangerously arched eyebrow. "I'm *always* trying to help you. I stay home from parties 'cause you're too scared to go."

"I'm not—"

"I totally blow off Jeremy to hang out with you so you won't spend all your time moping. I even share my *parents* with you when your own dad can't take care of you."

"Don't talk about my dad," I snap, my fists clenched at my sides.

"Then don't call me stupid."

"You're the dumbest dumbass in the world if you think you know anything about me or my family."

She's smiling now, so cold you could catch frostbite.

I've seen this smile turned on those second-floor-bathroom girls, but never on me. Every word in her oversweet voice is like an icicle shattering on the hardwood floor. "You should probably go home, then. Lindy's, like, a genius, right? Maybe she'll be a better only-friend."

So I leave. As soon as I numbly wave good-bye to Mr. Price and Dr. Van Tassel, who are busy in the kitchen, pretending they didn't hear a word of our fight, I'm out the door and running, hot-faced, sweating through my stupid puffy coat even in the bitter, damp cold, past lit yellow windows and fancy gated lawns. I don't stop till I'm slamming in through my own front door. I don't even have time to shed my bag and coat before Lindy's in my face.

"What is it? What's wrong?"

"Nothing," I try to snap. It comes out more like a gasp, my breath shredded from the brief sprint, from force-swallowing the lump in my throat.

"Imogene," she says desperately, following me through the living room.

"Leave me *alone*, Lindy," I warn her.

"Immy, I can't do that." She swoops in front of me. "Something's obviously going on with you. I know you're scared."

"No, I'm *not*."

"I know how worried you are about your dad. Lord knows I am." She grabs for my stiff fingers. "But I'm asking you not to shut me out. Not now, when we're depending on each other. Josh would want us to—"

"I don't need a fucking therapist, Lindy." I tear my hand away. "Nobody in this house does!"

The corners of her carefully painted poppy-red lips wobble. "That's all that I am to you?"

As Lindy's face blurs in front of me, I can't stop myself from saying what I know I shouldn't say: "That's what you *are*. I don't need your stupid talks, and I don't need you, and neither does my dad!" I reach out and push, and my thin-boned stepmother stumbles into the wall at the foot of the stairs.

Lindy's whisper is a whip crack between us. "Please go to your room, Imogene."

"You can't—"

"Yes, I can. Maybe I'm not the parent you want, but I'm what you've got. So go to your room." She no longer seems on the verge of tears, and if she would look me in the eye, I suspect I'd see nothing but careful composure.

Except she won't look at me.

Why should she? Not only am I pathetic, I'm mean. And I'm the dumbass for truly believing that just because my real mother didn't want me, she needed saving.

But this isn't helping me find the only person who I

now know really needs me: my dad.

What I do is, once I'm safe in my room, door appropriately slammed, and I've flopped facedown on my faded bedspread, I imagine my heart in my chest. I imagine prying it open with a chisel and rock hammer, and once it splits down the seam I push out Lindy and Chad and Jessa, one by one. I fit the halves back together after them and tell myself I'll learn to love the quiet they leave behind. I don't need a stepmother, I don't need a boyfriend, and I really don't need a best friend.

Dad's taught me a lot over the years: how to pick the lock on my old Civic, how to choose the best table at Subway. How to read. How to make a Bloody Mary. How to swim and how to breathe out and sink. How to find a woman with only a seventeen-year-old picture in the back of a mystery book and a bedtime story as clues—and I did that much at least.

But if there's one thing Dad's bad times have taught me, it's this: I never, ever want to have anything I can't survive without.

SIXTEEN

Wednesday morning, I wake up to a horrible raw ache—like Monday's hangover but full-bodied—and Lindy standing over my bed.

"Where are your keys, Imogene?"

"What?" I mumble into my pillow. I slide my head up and feel something grind into my chest: the stone heart, crystal-side down on the mattress, trapped under me while I slept.

"Your keys. Car and house. Are they in your bag?" By the sound of her perfectly measured voice, she hasn't forgiven me.

I nod once and pull the comforter over my head, watching through a peephole between the blanket and the mattress.

Going literally undercover doesn't stop Lindy from monologuing while she roots through my bag. Keys jingle as she pries them out of the front pouch and tucks them in her blazer pocket. "I really wanted us to be a team, but things have to change around here. You've been running around without telling me, without asking permission, hardly checking in. You won't talk to me at all. Phone?" she asks, and despite my silence spots my cell phone on the charger on my nightstand. She pockets that, too. "I don't know what to do with you, Imogene. I don't know how to convince you that I'm the parent and you're the child." Lindy crosses to my desk and unplugs my laptop, which she tucks beneath her arm. "I'm working late, and then I have my meeting with Officer Griffin. She wants to get together once a week, until this is all . . . over. I'm going to tell her I want us to go the media. Get this on the news and online. It's time we face facts that your father isn't going to drift back in and make everything all right on his own steam. I'll be home before nine, and if you'd like to *talk* to me then, we'll figure out what to do and where to go from here. You can spend the day at home, thinking about what you want to say to me."

Though my own breath stales the air beneath the blankets, I wait until I hear Lindy leave my room, descend, and go out through the garage door. Not until I hear her car rumble to life and pull away do I come out.

I listen to the wind whistling through the cracks in the house and massage the spot below my collarbone where the stone definitely left a bruise. I remember taking it to bed with me, staring into the center of it until I fell asleep. I remember thinking maybe I've been wrong this whole time. Maybe it never meant anything that Dad left it for me. Maybe I've been just as crazy as he is, thinking this was some kind of mystery I was capable of solving, when really he's god knows where in god knows what kind of shape.

I bury myself under the blankets again. Let Lindy take everything away. Who's left to talk to? Where is there left to go? Why even bother getting out of bed? All those times I left Dad's room, defeated, having failed to unearth him from his sheets—maybe he was onto something.

Then I sit up as I remember the last decision I made before falling asleep: to have faith in the one thing that matters. The one thing I *know*.

My dad is still out there, and he needs me to do my job. To take care of him.

After that, I move slowly. First I roll out of the sheets

and boil myself pink under a too-hot shower. Then I take the time to dry my hair with a clunky hand-me-down blow dryer from Lindy, so it won't freeze around me in the cold. I even dig out my makeup bag. Usually I skim from the top layer of cake-flavored ChapStick and, if I'm feeling ambitious, my un-daring and inexpertly applied brown eyeliner. This time I dig deeper for the works, a disk of blush, and even a tube of red lipstick, a castoff from Jessa I've always chickened out of using. Now I trace my mouth like I'm coloring with a crayon, slowly, then smack my lips the way Jessa's fabulous aunt Annette taught us and lean in toward the mirror.

I try to feel the way I felt in the Prices' bathroom, preparing to track down Lillian Eugene: unstoppable, armored, badass. But in the toothpaste-spackled mirror I'm puffy-eyed and still pale, with red wax lips. Quickly I scrub my failed attempt off with a tissue.

To stand in front of the bathroom sink and stare at myself is to stop moving, so I give up and get dressed in my warmest sweater and a decent pair of jeans. I pull on my woolen socks and a fuzzy winter hat Jessa bought me two birthdays ago, the one that looks like a strawberry with a green pom-pom for the stem. Just before stuffing myself into my puffy coat, gloves, and winter boots, I do a preflight check on the contents of my bag:

Dad's hardcover copy of *A Time to Chill*.

The stack of photos and the MFA brochure from Lil.

Todd Malachai's phone number and address—56 Pines Road, Windham, Connecticut—copied over from the smudged numbers still glittering on my palm.

The leftover cash from Lindy's envelope: $92.03, after a tank of gas and the useless prom dress, which I'm now viciously regretting.

When everything seems in order, I zip my jacket up to the collar, turn the latch on the front door, and lock myself out, into a bright winter day. There's a loose screen I can jiggle off the track to break in through the unlatched window in the back of the house if I get home before Lindy. (And if I don't, I'll probably lose the privilege to close the bathroom door while I take a crap.)

Then I start walking.

It takes me forty minutes to make it the two miles to the train and bus station on East Main. The whole way my boots slip over black ice on the sidewalks, and the wind frosts my jeans to my legs so that by the time I tramp snow onto the green marble tiles of Sugarbrook station, the denim has scraped my frozen skin raw. I pull off my gloves and fumble open the zipper of my coat with clawed hands.

For another thirty-eight dollars, I buy a round-trip ticket with a last stop at a Cumberland Farms/Peter Pan bus stop in Willimantic, which the guy who rings me up assures me is a (not-so-nice) part of Windham. The bus doesn't leave until noon and won't get me to Willimantic until three thirty, so I plop down on a bench behind the elevated wooden platform where they put up holiday displays—a miniature cobwebbed graveyard for Halloween, a piano-size cornucopia overflowing with papier-mâché gourds and grapes and turkeys for Thanksgiving. Around Christmastime, Dad used to take me to the station every year to see the decorations. They put up a model of Sugarbrook with a toy railroad around it. Not as big as they do in Boston, but super detailed. There's a set of palm-size, whitewashed buildings on the east and west sides of town representing Sugarbrook High and J. Jefferson Agricultural. There's the ring of brick businesses and the Patty Linden Memorial Park, as big as a chessboard, studded with plastic paper birches, with a miniature stone fountain that really trickles water. There's Christy Pond, an oval of rippled green glass with toy paddleboats moored at the dock. Pylons like matchsticks poke up where the old pier rotted away before I was born. A pretty accurate web of suburban homes spins out from the town center; there's even a street Dad and I decided was Cedar Lane. On one end are the delicate little mansions and on the other, wee cookie-cutter houses. Though the town isn't copied inch by inch, there's a middle-size home in the middle of the street we declared to be our own. Pale blue instead of pale green, but with a tiny picket fence like ours. Each year, we would lean over the rope around the platform and stare into the miniature electric-lit window, watching for miniature us living out our miniature lives.

For Lindy's First Christmas with Us (Dad referred to it in Capital Letters) he tried to get us all down to the station to see it. Except my brand-new stepmother had to work, and then we went on a painful holiday visit to magnificent Pahaquarry, New Jersey, to meet my new stepfamily. By the time we got around to Sugarbrook station it was January, and they were tearing down the town. Trees uprooted all over, polka-dotting the Astroturf with empty sockets. Blue and green wires tangling out of the dry park fountain. Paddleboats overturned on the dusty glass pond. And the houses—most were gone by then, whirled away to Oz (or the Sugarbrook station basement). I didn't even bother peeking at mini Cedar Street.

The next year Dad got Lindy to the station on time, but I stayed out of it. This year and last, we missed it completely. By now the display is long gone. I guess they've just taken down their Valentine's Day setup, because the pink glitter still speckles the platform planks.

I kill the hour-and-a-half wait by rereading *A Time to Chill* for the eleventy-hundredth time and plowing through vending machine packages of peanut butter crackers and mini cookies. My prom fund is rapidly depleting, though I should have plenty for a taxi from the bus stop to Todd Malachai's and back, with cash left over. The return trip is a little shorter and I actually stand a chance of beating Lindy home, depending on how long she spends with Officer Griffin at the police station. If not, maybe I can lie and say I went to Jessa's to make nice. I'll probably have to add that it didn't go so great.

Before I know it, my bus is boarding. I settle into a seat in the rear, pull the hood of my coat up, curl inward around Dad's book, and accept that there's no turning back.

Thankfully, I make both bus transfers in Springfield and in Hartford, Connecticut, and disembark outside the Cumberland Farms. The "bus stop" is a row of black iron benches outside the convenience store, gleaming with ice, and not a cab stand in sight. I've hung around Boston enough to know how to fish for taxis, but this isn't exactly the city. Beyond the parking lot is a street stuffed with two-family housing in a faded rainbow of unhealthy colors. I'm not even sure which direction to head to get to Pines Road, and I can't call a cab company.

All right, so it was fairly dumb to cross state lines without any kind of cell phone. Unsure of my next move, I stand on the sidewalk and tuck my chin into my jacket. It's no warmer in Windham than in Sugarbrook, and as a bonus there's a cold, ripe fog, the sky dull even though sunset is hours away.

The only thing I can think to do is retreat into the little yellow-lit store. I wait in line behind a woman buying yogurt raisins and lottery tickets to talk to the clerk, a boy about Chad's age. Watching me through bleary eyes, he drones, "Can I help you?"

Everyone is always asking me that.

"I was wondering, how do I hail a cab around here?"

"Have to call one, I think. Try Ace Taxi Service. You gonna buy something?"

I lean in toward him the way Pari Singh leaned into Chad, draping my hip against the counter, propping one elbow on the conveyer belt. "See, that's the problem. I don't have a phone on me, so I *can't* call. But if you've got a phone . . . I'm really stuck, you know?" I can't possibly replicate the Pari effect, not with my hideous coat, my strawberry hat, my puffy eyes and raw lips.

"My phone's in the back room. Are you gonna buy something, or what?"

The old man behind me coughs pointedly, rearranges his bags of chips on the belt.

I straighten, defeated. "Look, just . . . please? Please, can you help me?"

He curls his bottom lip, fuzzed with a feeble little soul patch. "Whatever. I got a break in twenty. Have to hang around till then. Now can you get out of line?"

So I loiter in the canned-goods aisle until Shaggy from *Scooby-Doo* takes his break, and use his phone to call a cab while he taps his foot impatiently on the tile floor, pack of cigarettes and lighter in hand.

When the taxi arrives it takes me to Pines Road, which is actually a condo complex. Identical peach-colored two-stories snake around the development. It looks nice here. Nice and neat, with perfectly flat-topped shrubs below each white shuttered window, and a fancy knocker on every door. Old-fashioned lampposts at the foot of each walkway look like miniature, twinkly brass houses.

The ride costs me $14.45 and I peel off a two-dollar tip, thinning my bankroll even further. Before I climb out of the taxi I ask for the time.

"Around four," the driver says, checking out number fifty-six through his passenger side window. "Doesn't look like anyone's home," he says. "Want me to wait till you get inside? It's starting to snow."

I shake my head and pull my gloves on. "No, thanks. I'll be okay."

The whole trip down I was wondering how it'd feel to ring the doorbell, but it's not a problem. Even before I cup my hands and peer through the glass of the side window into the dark beyond the door, I can tell there's no one home.

So I sit down a front stoop identical to the front stoops around it, sheltered from the snow by an over-hanging (and pristine) gutter, and I wait.

And wait.

I don't know for how long. The already-dark sky darkens further, and snow powders the shrubs around me until they're white-capped, and I have to cross my legs and run my hands briskly over my jeans to keep the blood in them. To distract myself I dig into my bag, meaning to pull out Dad's book but landing on the MFA brochure instead.

With shivering hands, I flip to the picture of my mother and try to untangle the little knot of hurt I feel when I look at her.

All this time. She's been all across Massachusetts—and beyond!—and still when it came to it, I managed to track her down quick enough. Here I am one week later, freezing on her front stoop.

Meanwhile, I've been in the same house my whole life. We've never changed our phone number. For god's sake, we never change the magnets on the fridge.

I don't really care about her, I tell myself. I don't feel this way because I miss her. I don't even know her. I only miss the family I've been imagining since I was six years old and first heard my bedtime story; the family we will never be. And that kind of missing hangs around like the pain of a rotten tooth, throbbing when it's knocked against. Maybe this is horrible, but that was okay, I figured, as long as somewhere out there, she was in pain too.

I could forgive my mother for being cursed, and lonely, and troubled waters. All of that made sense. But I don't think I'll be able to forgive her if she's happy.

After a while, after my fingers have stiffened around the paper and drifting snowflakes have dampened and bled spots of ink, a car pulls up and parks in front of number fifty-six. A tall black man in a crisp trench coat and red knit cap climbs out.

I think about sweeping off my strawberry hat so I'll be taken seriously, but I'm not sure I could raise my arms high enough if I wanted. While I'm weighing my options, the man shuffles up the front walk, head down against the snow. Flakes cling to his cap and the shoulders of his coat. Fishing his keys out of his pocket, he stops just in front of the stoop. "Can I help you?"

My lips are numb, and I have to scrub my gloved fingers across them to get them warm and working. "I'm waiting," I chatter, "for Sidonie. She lives here, doesn't she?"

He squints against the wind as snowflakes pearl his long eyelashes. "How long you been out here?"

I twitch my shoulders upward.

"Okay, but . . . I think you'd better wait inside. It'll be a little while. She's at her class." Unlocking the front door, he chuckles and says, "You're not a process server or an assassin or anything, are you?"

"I'm actually kind of her long-lost daughter?" I try to throw my arms up casually, like, What can you do? but my limbs are so stiff with cold and my winter gear so constricting, they just flop fishlike by my sides.

He blinks at me, frozen, one boot through the door. "Seriously?"

SEVENTEEN

While Todd Malachai stuffs our winter gear into the closet, I stand in the doorway to the living room and examine their home.

It's cozy. Artsy. The walls are a warm color that makes me think of caramel drizzled on ice cream. In no particular line or order, big paintings splatter the walls. Animals, forests, beaches. Most are impressionistic. Above the brown leather couch there's a horse with a bulbous head, like you're looking at it from inside a fish bowl. All over, there are green cotton-ball trees and oceans so choppy, they're triangular. I put my nose up to the closest painting and read the scratchy signature in the corner of the frame.

"They're Sid's." Todd comes up beside me. "She's in her art class now. Just a little group they got going on the college campus. Meets Wednesday evenings . . . but I digress. So. You'd be Joshua's daughter?"

Shocked, I turn to him. "Do you know my dad?"

"Oh, no. I didn't mean . . . I just, I knew Sid had a past before we . . . How did you find us? Not that—I'm not sorry you did. I'm not . . ." He spreads his arms. "I'm not too sure what to say. Never been in a situation quite like this."

I give him a weak smile.

"Some tunes while we wait?" He crosses to a bookshelf next to the couch and bends over a sleek black box on one of the shelves. With a long finger he presses a button, and a lid pops open, revealing a record player like the Prices have, though theirs hangs on the wall in their den. Todd thumbs through a stack of records beside it, plucks one out, and slides it below the needles. Fast saxophone ripples over the speakers. "Art Pepper." He holds up the sleeve. "One of the greatest. Don't suppose you're a fan of West Coast jazz?"

"Um, not really." I reach out and touch the frosted-glass shade of a lamp on the side table, pluck a tile coaster with a big M on it off the neat stack next to the lamp. It's cold and heavy in my hand. "Dad's a classic-rock guy. Twisted Sister and stuff. He calls it hair metal."

"He seems like a cool guy," Todd says. It occurs to me that technically speaking, I'm talking to my stepfather. I resolve at once not to like him, though that resolve mushifies when he asks, "You hungry, Imogene? I was just about to make myself a snack."

All I've had since dinner last night was the fistful of vending machine crackers and mini cookies. I can feel my stomach grumbling at the mention of food. "I'm fine."

He shakes his head. "That's too bad. I don't think I can eat the whole box of pizza bites myself. At least join me for moral support."

Their kitchen is small and buttery yellow and smells like cinnamon, which could just be an air freshener, but makes me hungrier anyhow. *My mother cooks in this kitchen.* Todd shakes frozen pizza bites onto a foiled cookie sheet, and pops a whole second tray of spicy pot stickers into the oven without asking me. I touch the handle of the silverware drawer. *My mother eats yogurt with the spoons she keeps in here.* It all seems preposterous.

"You like cranberry juice?" he asks. I nod, inspecting my technically-stepfather-who-definitely-isn't-likable-or-handsome while he roots around in the fridge. Except he is handsome. Gone is the old flat-top haircut of prom night. Now his curly black hair is shaved close, sprinkled with gray. His skin is rich red-brown, and a light blue sweater tugs across his broad shoulders when he grabs a bottle from the back of the fridge. I remember that he's years younger than Dad, and if his shoulders are a little less stooped, why shouldn't they be? He got the girl.

He plunks a glass down on the counter in front of me. "Does someone know you're here? I don't suppose your father dropped you off. I don't even know how you made it out here."

"It . . . took a long time," I settle on.

"I'll bet. We're kind of in the sticks. Is there anyone you want to check in with?"

I take a nervous sip of juice, wishing for the courage of a Captain and Coke about now. "When will Sidonie be home, do you know?"

"They usually wrap up around six. It won't be long now."

The clock on the microwave blinks 5:47. If I were to leave now, catch a ride from Todd to the Quick Mart, I might even make the six o'clock bus—my last chance to beat Lindy home, no harm, no foul. "I can wait."

"I figured." He nods. "So. What shall we talk about

in the meantime?" He smiles, but in a likable way, unfortunately.

I ask him to tell me about my mother, of course, so he does. He tells me how they met—how they met again—about five years back. He was visiting his niece, a dancer with the Nutmeg Ballet in Torrington. He would've left town right after the matinee show, but his niece begged him to stay and take her to dinner, so he did. On his way out of town, he stopped at a gas station for cigarettes (he was a chimney stack of a smoker back then, he assures me). And who should be paying for her gas in cash at the counter but his old high school girlfriend Sidonie Faye, all grown up. Even though Todd had a long drive ahead of him and had already eaten dinner, even though it was a Sunday and he had work early the next morning at this mattress store in Fitchburg, he asked her to come eat with him without a second thought. They hadn't seen each other in maybe twenty years, and he'd always missed her, always wondered what happened to her when she left for school and never came home.

They talked. A lot. She told him that while studying abroad—

"In Sweden or Switzerland?" I interrupt.

He scratches his chin and guesses it was one of those S-countries. Anyway, a letter had found its way to her from Boston, battered and much rerouted. It told her that her mother had died, that Sidonie was needed to come claim the body. That's how she found herself back in the States, alone. One of those girls determined never to look back once she left their dinky little hometown and less-than-perfect childhood, she'd broken off with all her friends from high school, and the only surviving family in the area was a cousin she'd fallen out of touch with. She felt like she was floating, unattached to the place that had been her home, and too upset to go back to her life abroad. Then, when there was no one else, the forensic pathologist who'd worked on her mother was there, of all people. My dad helped my mother find a part-time job at the museum through a friend of a friend, a way to use the art degree she'd abandoned. He even helped her find a place to stay in Boston, a little apartment with a garden on the building roof. He was older than her, but soon enough they were together. When she felt her depression closing in, this dark cloud she'd struggled to outrun all her life, he convinced her to leave the city with him. A small, slow town in the suburbs would be good for them, he said.

Here in the story, Todd winces as the egg timer bleats beside the stove. He stops to extract the baking sheets.

"What about me?" I ask, hopping up onto the counter, the way Lindy hates. *Do you think it's wise to put your backside where we slice tomatoes?* she always asks. But this way I'm eye-level with Todd Malachai, and I doubt he's going to yell at me. "Did she ever even tell you she had a daughter?" I search his face for the truth.

He looks away. "No. If she had, we'd have gone from there. But I never asked. I suppose I guessed, though, because of the sketchbook."

"What sketchbook?"

"You'll see when your mother gets here."

While the food cools and my stomach consumes itself over the smell, Todd tells the rest of the story.

When my mother left Sugarbrook—and she was never very clear on why she'd left, or how or when— she stayed with a work friend, then after she quit her job, a new boyfriend, and another after that. They never lasted or made much of an impression, and none were very good to her. ("One was in a band, and *not* a jazz band," Todd adds.) Eventually she left the state entirely, and landed in Torrington. While she crumbled crackers into her soup in a little diner, my mother confessed to Todd Malachai that she felt she was floating once again. Lost. Todd told her if she ever came back to Fitchburg, she'd have a friend. He could help her, and coming home might be good for her. There was even a new place in town, a place his brother-in-law had gone in the months after he was laid off.

She thanked him, insisted on splitting the bill, and left. He never thought he'd see her again, until a month later when she was knocking on his door, telling him that she'd quit her job, that she was finally, really ready to get help.

"And what, she just barnacled on to you?" I sneer. "You take her in, and she takes your money and crashes your truck?"

"Huh?" He frowns.

"Your great-aunt Hilda told me about her."

Todd surprises me by laughing. "Oh, no! That wasn't your mother. You really did your research, though, huh? God, Aunt Hilda was thinking of Jen Lavato. Surprised she remembered her. That girl was a piece of work. I was dumb to run around with Jenny. My dad hated her, called me a fool. He was right. That was something like a decade ago, before he died."

Hilda said as much, thinking back. Of course, if I was any kind of actual detective instead of a stupid kid pretending, I might've seen the truth, and not the story I wanted to be true.

"It wasn't that kind of thing with your mom," Todd continues. He hands me an overfull plate and leans back against the counter, contemplating a pizza bite. "She wouldn't take anything from me. I told her I had a spare room above the garage, but she insisted on paying rent, and paying for enrollment at New Hope. Said her cousin had sent her some money and helped her out."

Now I know why Mom called Lilian Eugene asking for cash after all those years apart.

"But you weren't, like, together?"

"Not for a while. Not until she got help, and said she felt strong enough for a new start. She had a job offer here in Windham—one of the doctors at New Hope connected her with a lawyer friend looking to hire an assistant. She asked me to come with her, so I did. She proposed to me last year."

"How romantic."

We stuff our faces in silence for a while, and after refilling my plate for me, he starts up, "Normally I wouldn't be telling you her story like this, Imogene. I'd say it was hers to tell. But you're probably carrying around a lot of real hurt. That's natural. I just wanted . . . I'm explaining so you'll give her a chance. Try to listen to her. She's had a hard life."

"I *really* don't care." I shove my twice-emptied plate away.

Just then the front door opens and quickly shuts, and a woman's voice calls out from the far room. "Sweetie? Sorry I'm late. Traffic was a bitch in the snow."

"We're in here!" he shouts back, watching me. I try

to keep a blank face, but I can feel the blood draining out of it, pounding straight into my heart. I wipe my suddenly sweaty palms on the hem of my sweatshirt and try to find a pose that says Fuck you, *world*. I settle for sitting up straight on the counter and crossing my arms to stop myself from cracking my knuckles.

"Who is 'we'?" And then my mother is standing in the kitchen doorway.

Ticking my head to the side, I examine her: a small, thin woman with lots of mouse-brown hair waving down to her elbows. Framed by all that hair is a small heart-shaped face. Big hazel eyes under pointed brows. Thin lips that rest in a kind of amused miniature smile. Under one arm she carries a big drawing pad. Her coat is off, but a flouncy blue scarf is tucked under her narrow chin. My chin.

"Hi, Mom." It comes out rough and dry, like the sound of Dad rasping a hand down his unshaved cheek.

"I knew it," she whispers. "After the phone call. Imogene? How . . . ?"

"Oh." I shrug. "You know. I broke into a hospital. Stole your medical files. Tracked down your cousin. Phony-called your old boss. Got money for a fake prom. Talked to your old neighbor. Found your husband's address. Took a bus."

One delicate eyebrow shoots upward. "You knew how to do all that?"

"I read a lot."

When she and I are seated at opposite ends of the kitchen table, Todd kisses her temple through the curtain of her hair. Illuminated in the chandelier light from above, it's not as dark as it seemed in pictures, but a kind of dirty blond.

He sets down a glass of juice in front of my mother (she had no interest in pizza bites or pot stickers) and says, "I'm going out. See if old Mrs. Walters doesn't need help salting her front walk. You two . . . call if you need anything." There's the shuffle of fabric as he zips on layers in the front hallway, and then he's gone. Aside from gnawing on her thumbnail, my mother's been frozen since Todd sat her down in her seat, but at the sound of the door she comes to life again. She starts to slide the drawing pad under the table.

"Can I see?" I ask.

She pauses, then hands me the pad, as long as my arm at least, and as I flip through the sketches I try to look as if I don't care, like I'm just checking eggs in a carton for breaks, the way I do when I grocery shop for me and Dad. They're good, though none of them are complete. Like, on one page is a woman's face and breasts and belly, perfectly realistic, then just a brown chalk squiggle where her spine should be. In another, flat blocks of all colors make up a man's body, and at the end of two straight stalk arms, two beautifully detailed and shaded hands. Here is an older woman's finely drawn head perched on a simple pear-shaped outline of a body. There, two feet stick out from a long cloud of blue chalk.

"Do you draw?" she asks me.

I close the pad and shove it away from me. "No. I write. Like Dad." Not exactly true, but I'm going for the wound here.

She nods. "I bet. That's good. I read his books, you know? A couple of them. You look like him, too." She stares across the table at me and I know what she sees: the dark, flat hair, the Asian stamp of my features, the downward curve of my lips, like his. She sighs and folds her hands in front of her. They're small, but not delicate or anything. The fingers are slim, but the knuckles are round like bolts, the skin chapped and callused. They're the oldest-looking part of her. "Whatever you came to say to me, I deserve."

"You have no idea what I came for."

If she's stung by my words, she doesn't show it. "I'm guessing it wasn't to give me a World's Best Mom mug."

She laughs, and it's an empty sound. "I know Todd filled you in on my story, but I'm guessing it doesn't help much. I wasn't there with you. I should've been, but I couldn't do it. I wasn't well. I know that now. I wanted to be better for you."

This is it. My chance to ask the big question, the all-consuming, zero-room-for-anything-else-until-the-mystery-is-solved question, which I always thought would be a simple one: *Why did you leave Sugarbrook?* But what comes out surprises me: "So why couldn't you be better?"

She reaches for her glass, stares into it but doesn't drink. "I don't know."

"That's not an answer."

"I want to give you what you need, Imogene, but there just isn't an easy answer. Sometimes it's chemicals, or shitty memories. Life wasn't easy with my mom . . . even before she left. And sometimes it just *is*. On and off my whole life, it's been that way. Before you came along, I guess I *was* miserable. Part of it was Mom's death. But I hadn't even really known her. . . ." Here, she looks up at me through her eyelashes, then quickly away. "And it didn't start with her. Then time went by and there wasn't even sadness.

"You know how another patient put it? She said this feeling inside her was . . . it was anti-feeling. Like a black hole in space, and everything—happiness, anger, hope, meaning—it would all get sucked in, tipped over the event horizon, and she couldn't feel any of it. That's the way it was for me. I walked around like everyone else, and had this wonderful opportunity at the museum, and came home to this brilliant guy who loved me and was nothing but sweet. Your father tried so hard. But I felt . . . empty. If I could've filled that space up with anything, I would've. If somebody had turned to me and said, 'It's easy, just pour some dry cement in there and you'll be a normal human girl,' I would've done it like that." She snaps her fingers. "But I couldn't. And your father couldn't do it for me. Then . . . then I was pregnant, and it all happened so fast. I was only twenty-one, and we weren't even seriously talking marriage! But I thought . . ."

"I would fix you?" I finish the sentence, and she doesn't deny it. "Maybe you should've gotten a dog or something. Eased into it."

Her thin mouth twists.

What did I expect from the elusive Sidonie Faye? One single, perfect answer to all the questions I've ever had, all the mother-daughter days I've missed, all the nights I've stayed up wondering if I was cursed like my mom and her mom before her, if I was doomed to turn into a woman who could be lonely wherever she went?

Those sorts of answers exist, I suppose. But only in stories.

"So. You left us in the middle of the night and never came back. Never called. Never sent a Valentine's Day card. Not even now that you're blissfully happy and married and in freaking art class."

Her swollen knuckles are white around her juice glass. "I was terrified. I knew you'd hate me. I was afraid to hear I'd ruined your life."

"My life was fine. We were just fine without you. Almost like nothing was missing," I lie, assembling one arched eyebrow and a slight sneer into Jessa's trademark mask of icy disinterest, usually reserved for enemies.

"I hoped you would be okay," Sidonie answers in a small voice, looking down through the curtain of her hair. All at once, it's like she's the kid and I'm the grown-up.

I like it that way. I want to keep control while I have it—it's better than letting in the old rotten-tooth pain. "It doesn't matter. I didn't come so you could apologize. I already knew pretty much everything before I came. There are just a couple questions I have, and then I'm leaving." Might as well go for the big one right off, though by now I don't expect to get much out of it. With a deep breath, I ask, "When was the last time you spoke with my dad?"

"About a week ago, I guess? No. Exactly a week ago, actually."

I can feel every muscle in my body seize up and stiffen, my heart leading the charge. "Seriously? You're telling me you spoke with him?"

She hesitates, chewing on her thumbnail and its chipped blue polish. "Not directly. But I thought you knew. I thought that was why you came to see me. Imogene, what's going on here?"

"Just, please tell me what he said."

"It was a message he left on our machine. Last Thursday. Todd was already gone—he had an early department meeting. I got out of the bathroom and saw the machine blinking, so . . ." She chomps on her nail again. "I hadn't heard from him in so long. He used to send letters, and sometimes they got to me, but I never wrote back. Then, there his voice was, coming out of the speakers. He said he wanted us to meet."

"On Valentine's Day," I finish.

"Yes, I guess it was. He told me he needed to see me and he'd be waiting for me by the water. That was it." She shrugs helplessly.

"So what did you do about it?"

"What could I do? He didn't leave a number. And I couldn't leave my husband to traipse around every body of water in Massachusetts."

I'm not so much listening to her excuses as digging through Dad's message. By the water? Did he mean the Charles River in Boston? It's not far from Good Shepherd Hospital. Or did he mean . . .

"Do you think he could be talking about Victory Island?"

"Oh my god." Her eyes are hazel moons. "I haven't thought about that place in almost twenty years. We only went once, you know? We stumbled onto it on a long drive and stayed the night in this hotel down by the shore. This silly little tourist trap, the cheapest place on the beach I bet. The room was such a laugh. It had this Hawaiian theme. But as soon as we walked into the lobby, I knew it was the right place to be."

"And it was important to you guys?"

"It was where we, um, decided to . . . keep the baby. You. That was the whole point of the big, long drive. To decide what to do." She nods. "It was important. I even kept our old room key. They were still using keys then, you know? I bet I still have it in my jewelry box."

Jesus. This whole time. The police drove out there and found nothing, and neither did Lindy and I. Then again, how could I have? I was so convinced he was running toward my mother and not holed up alone, I didn't even really look for him. Besides, the beach was our place and belonged to us, to my dad and me. At least, I thought it did.

The list of what I *know* is shrinking by the second.

I want to walk right out the door and not stop until I get to Victory Island, but that would be stupid beyond stupid. It turns out I've been a fairly bad detective thus far, so I have to get serious. A good detective would get all the information she could before running off. Reaching into the bag at my feet, I extract the stone heart and place it gem-side-up on the kitchen table. It rolls slowly along its curve until it's tilted, winking at my mother in the chandelier light from above.

"Where on earth did you get that?" She leans for a closer look and hugs herself, fingertips digging into her arms.

"From my dad. I want to know where he got it and what it means."

"It was my mother's," she says, and crazily, my pulse skips a beat. "I had a collection of these things when I was a kid. My father worked for this company—they made screws for everything. Jewelry, ovens, vending machines, just everything. They would send him to visit their big buyers and he'd always bring one of these back for me. Geodes, I think they're called. I don't know why he started, but he went away enough that I had drawers of them. But this one"—she reaches out and brushes the rind of stone around the crystals with an index finger, and it rolls on its axis—"they found in her coat pocket when she died. The police thought maybe she was on her way to Fitchburg . . . or on her way from. I don't know."

"She was bringing it to you?" I ask.

My mother leans back in her chair. "Maybe. It was too late. I wasn't there anymore, so she never found me."

"Dad said you took the other half with you when you left us.".

"I did, but that, I don't have anymore. It's back home." She flinches. "In Fitchburg, I mean. That's where my parents are buried."

I hate to ask anything else, because I'm still trying to pretend I don't care about anything but Dad. But I came all this way. "Would you ever have tried to find me? I mean . . . I thought you were a total broken mess, but here you have this, like, perfect life. Did you just forget about me?"

She gives me this pitying look, and it makes me feel like the kid again. "Imogene, you don't *just forget* your daughter. There were times when I had to fight, every damn day, just to be here. I wish I'd gotten help sooner. But sometimes, all I could do was . . . I would draw."

"Monsters, right? Made-up shit?" I think of Lil and my mother in their tent in that tangled backyard, of the shredded butcher paper balled up and stuffed in my garbage can at home.

Silently, she rises and leaves the kitchen. After a few minutes I think I've chased her away for good, and I'm not sure how to feel about that. But she comes back in and thumps a sketchbook down on the table. A thick cream one, much smaller than her drawing pad, bound like any book, with a deep seam down the spine. The cover's splattered with pen and paint and god knows what else. It looks like my much-abused copy of *Rebecca*. She slides it across to me. I waver for a second before opening it.

Inside are drawings of little girls. Except they're not all little. There are babies, and toddlers, and kindergarten-age girls and school-age girls and teenagers. After studying them, I realize they're actually all the same girl, just at different ages. And they're all familiar. They all look sort of like me.

Not exactly like me. The toddler is chubby and smiling, where I was thin and always looked a little angry/creepy, thanks to the frowny mouth. The ten-or-so-year-old has too-long hair and a ski-slope nose like Sidonie and wears braids, which I never did. Dad didn't know how to braid. And the teenager is infinitely more stylish, and doesn't have my kind of pear shape. They've all got thinner lips than mine, and the teenager's hands look like smoother, younger versions of Sidonie's.

These drawings aren't of me, but of the way my mother imagined I might be. And there are pages and pages and pages of them. A whole book of them.

I paw at my eyes with the back of my hand.

Sidonie takes the book from me and slowly reaches for my arm, like she's afraid I'll jump away. "Were you really, honestly all right? Were you telling the truth when you said you and your dad were okay on your own?" Her eyes are huge in her small face. "You don't have to make me feel better. I don't deserve it."

I try to think of an answer, but instead I find myself thinking of handsome forensic pathologist Miles Faye. The first thing he tells you about himself is how he can read bodies like they're books. The plot of *A Time to Chill* kicks off with a simple, fascinating case that Miles solves easily. One of those gambits that shows us how brilliant he is, so that when the real mystery hits, we know it's a big deal. Seven be-suited businessmen are pulled from Boston Harbor on a winter night, the luxury cruiser they'd inexplicably rented for twilight sail having sunk miles out. Though they floated for a long time, the men were A-OK when they came out of the freezing water, chatting happily with the Coast Guard aboard the rescue boat, accepting cups of coffee. They went below decks to dry off and wrap up, and every one of the seven dropped down dead.

Miles looked at those blue-lipped bodies and knew immediately that:

1) All of the men had been drugged—by poisoned complimentary champagne aboard the rental boat, it later turned out, which is how they ended up in the water in the first place.

2) The men suffered from rewarming shock, wherein their icy hearts, once warmed, failed in the absence of blood. "The heart can take the cold," Miles said. "Sometimes it's the thaw that kills it."

The bodies told him everything he needed to know. And so when a crime comes along that he can't solve by looking, that's when the mystery begins.

There's no mystery when I look at my mother. The way she bites her thumbnail, the way she looks up at me through her eyelashes or, when she does turn away, the slight swing of her hair shielding her from view—in all of this, I can read the guilt and loneliness and sadness of the past, and how afraid she still is. I find every way I might hurt her. Everything I could say to smash the life she's built, to tear her apart where she's stitched herself together. The possibilities scroll through my mind and for a second, I think maybe there really are two kinds of girls, and I'm one of *those* girls: the kind who'll use what she knows to wound her mother in the worst way. To make her feel the way I felt when Dad was at his worst.

But no. I really don't think I am. At least, I don't want to be.

I smile, making sure it's a real one and not the icy kind my best friend uses to protect herself. "Yeah. We were okay. Dad . . . he wasn't perfect, but he was a really good dad."

It's true, after all. I had more than a lot of people have. More than Sidonie had when she was a little girl. I had Lindy, and Joshua Zhi Scott, who loved me so much and tried to be his best for me.

I think I can do this. I know it. If anyone can get him home, it's me, on my big shoulders.

EIGHTEEN

The outside world has changed in the past few hours. Thick snow coats the hedges and caps the ornate lamp-posts. Slowly, Todd backs his car up through inches of powder in the parking lot. As we pull away, a curtain resettles in the glowing window of 56 Pines Road.

Rather than leave me by a bench outside the Quick Mart, Todd insists on driving me all the way to Hartford, where I can catch my connection directly. It means a forty-minute drive with my mother's husband, but I don't mind so much. It's a quiet ride. Todd plugs in his MP3 player and lets me deejay, which gives us something to do besides talk about our pasts. I'm kind of over that subject, anyway. I shuffle through his favorites playlist, and by the time we pull up to the bright, bright lights of Union Station, I've been introduced to the best of West Coast jazz.

"Now, somebody will be waiting for you in Sugarbrook, yes?" he asks sternly as I collect my stuff.

One more lie. Just one more. Then I can take off my liar pants and pack them away, only break them out later for stuff like, *Don't worry, I haven't even been inside a boy's dorm room since I started college.* "My friend Jessa will be at the station," I promise. "She knows what time my bus gets in."

"Good. Don't be a stranger, all right? I'd give you our number, but I guess you already have it." He pats my puffy coat sleeve, and it's only slightly awkward.

"Right. Yeah. Thanks." I crack the door open, then on second thought, unbuckle the straps of my bag and pull out *A Time to Chill.* Letting it fall open to the bookmarked page, I peel off the battered sticky note holding my place and hand it to Todd. "Can you give this to Sidonie? It's her cousin's number. I think Lil would like it, you know, if they talked."

He tucks it into his pocket and grins. He has a nice smile. "You're really something else, aren't you, Imogene?"

If we had the time, I'd be in danger of liking my technical stepfather. We could compare favorite books. I could tell him about Dad's novels, and *The Hound of the Baskervilles*. *The Woman in White*. *Rebecca*.

Oh well. Maybe next time. "See you," I say, and shove out of the car into the snow.

At the Greyhound counter I buy a ticket to Boston. I know I can get to Victory Island from there—once, when Dad's car was in the shop, we rode the rail into Boston, switched from South Station to North Station, then took the Newburyport/Rockport Line. Just southeast of Newburyport, the tiny slice of land that makes up Victory Island juts out into the Atlantic, connected by one road to the mainland. It's maybe five miles from the station to the shoreline where hotels and motels overlook the water.

The ticket's another twenty-five dollars out of my fake-prom fund, and the train ride will probably be another ten dollars, which leaves me twenty-three dollars to flag a taxi to the island, and not nearly enough to get back home again. I'd better be right.

Because the next bus doesn't leave till eight thirty, I've got plenty of time to sit on a bench outside the Dunkin' Donuts kiosk and ponder the trouble I'm heaping on myself. Even if I can pull this off, I almost definitely shouldn't. Lindy will think I've run away like

Dad. It isn't right to do that to her.

There's still the nonrefundable, nonexchangeable return ticket I bought earlier that day that is set to take me from here to Framingham to Sugarbrook, though there's little chance that I could get home before Lindy. She'll be beyond furious that I left the house while grounded—correction, left the *state* while grounded. I'll be spending lunchtime in her office until I'm eating mashed bananas with dentures.

Risking my prime spot on the bench, I hustle over to the trash can and stuff my Sugarbrook ticket inside. With that decision symbolically made, I start rehearsing my speech for Dad, hoping I get the chance to make it tonight.

Mostly, trains are great. I've taken the rail lots of times with Dad, because it's even cheaper than parking in Boston, and often quicker than driving alongside Massholes at rush hour. The ride is even kind of peaceful. You can sit back and watch the trees blur by, and the fields, and the lakes like big silver coins. Trains are reliable and punctual; if the schedule says you'll be at Yawkey at 5:55 p.m., you'll probably be swimming upstream through the sweaty, noisy, beery crowds outside Fenway by six.

Except when it's really hot, and they slow the trains way down so the heat won't swell the steel and make the tracks all squiggly. Then again, they sometimes run late when it rains and an important patch of track floods, so everything has to shuffle around the water. And of course, there are delays when a conductor's out sick, or when a passenger falls down in the tiny bathroom and the whole line backs up for a medical emergency.

And when it's been snowing steadily all day, with six more inches set to fall before the weather clears in the early morning? Sometimes the trains stop completely.

I watch the big electronic boards at North Station flash CANCELED, CANCELED, CANCELED down the list. Most unfortunately, among them is the 10:40 train on the Newburyport/Rockport line, the last one that stops in Newburyport until the 6:30 a.m. train.

Dropping down on a bench far away from the drafty track doors, I look out on the flotsam of stranded people. There's a lot of frantic phone-calling, probably to best friends or parents or boyfriends. Some are stretching out on benches and in corners, buried deep inside the hoods of their coats, using backpacks as pillows. None of my (admittedly wobbly) plans involved spending the night in a big city train station. Even as I watch, it's clearing out, two Dunkin' Donuts and the Crazy Dough Pizza stand closed, McDonald's closing, stranded passengers flushing back out into the snow. I pull my bag into my lap and hug my knees to my chest. This is just the latest of at least a dozen rules I've broken in the What Girls Shouldn't Do Ever handbook. Still, I rip off my strawberry hat, pull up my hood, and settle in for a long night. It's just like sleeping in an airport, I tell myself, except slightly stupider.

Of course, I could still head to the payphone bank and call my stepmother to come get me. She'll never let me go to Victory Island, but I can convince her to call Officer Griffin. The police can find Dad; he could be home with us tomorrow night, everything put back the way it was.

And everything I have to say to him will have waited until I've lost the guts to say it, so it will never get said. We'll go on the same way we have been, till the next bad time.

I bury my hands in my pockets. Knocking past the geode, my fingertips find the greasy metal of the hotel room key. Sidonie gave it to me before I left Windham; I told her I wanted it, and she didn't complain.

The plain little key is light in my palm, with a yellowed plastic tag dangling from the cap. *The Tiki Motel*, it reads in swirly font. A silly, Hawaiian-themed motel that might be closed and condemned, for all I know. Maybe Dad's in a Super 8 somewhere along the shore. Or Dad isn't at Victory Island at all. Maybe he's waiting on a bench by a random duck pond in Malden. Or, Jesus, Miami Beach.

But no. Joshua Zhi Scott, after all, is a connect-the-dots, picture-in-the-stars kind of guy.

"Now arriving at . . . Newburyport," the pleasant, prerecorded voice over the train speakers wakes me up early on Thursday morning. Flinching in the glare of the just-risen sun, I slide upright against the cold window, toweling drool off my chin with my coat sleeve. Classy, Imogene. Pulling my gloves on, I squeeze down the aisle and spill out the doors onto the vaguely familiar concrete platform. A handful of shivering passengers shove roughly past me to get inside. I'm dead tired and hungry and cold, but I don't blame them. At least the snow has passed and the blue-gray sky is clear over the deserted parking lots that sandwich the platform.

Lindy must be awake in Sugarbrook—according to the train schedule, it's got to be seven thirty—but then again, I doubt she went to bed last night. She's going to slaughter me when I find my way home. I've broken so many rules, girl-specific and otherwise, that I wouldn't put it past her to have me homeschooled till graduation. Maybe home-colleged after that.

I pick my way across the messy sidewalks out onto Boston Way, where a few taxis idle. I knock on one window and ask if twenty bucks will get me to Victory Island. It will.

The lobby of the Tiki Motel is surprisingly spacious, but the brown-speckled carpeting and flowered yellow wallpaper aren't exactly elegant. Sidonie was right; the décor *is* a laugh. Over the front desk is a fake thatched roof, fake tropical birds pinned in the plastic straws. Artwork hangs on the walls, pictures of the sea in every size and color frame. I'm no expert—no assistant to the curator of prints and drawings—but none of it is museum quality. Except for one familiar print by the luggage cart. Small fishermen in a small boat on inky waters. A wistful dream of plentiful food. It seems unlikely that the place hasn't been remodeled in seventeen years, but my mother did say she knew straightaway that this was the place for them.

All of a sudden, it's depressing that this ridiculous tourist trap, which once meant so much to my parents and, I'm hoping, still means so much to Dad, never crossed her mind, not even after she heard his message. She really did leave us in the past.

The front desk clerk has his back to me, rooting around under the desk, and hasn't seen me yet. Betting he won't give out a guest's room number to just any uncombed teenager, I duck down a short hallway to my left, past the elevator and to the vending machine humming away at the end. Kicking off my boots and peeling off my coat, gloves, and hat, I stuff them and my bag into the corner beside the machine. With the last few coins in the bottom of my pocket I buy a Coke. I turn and survey my reflection in the tarnished gold doors, cloudy with handprints. I'm a static-haired, red-eyed mess, but it could work for me.

Shuffling out into the lobby in my socks, I call out, "Hi, um, excuse me?"

The clerk turns slowly. He looks exhausted. Probably worked the nightshift and won't be relieved till nine or so. Hopefully he won't give three craps about protocol this late in his shift.

"So, I locked myself out of my room?" I shrug and smile at him, channeling my inner Jessa. "I woke up and, like, came down to get a soda, but I forgot I lost my key card yesterday? And my dad's not answering the door? I think he's in the shower, maybe?"

"What room?" the clerk mutters, crossing to his computer.

"Umm . . . oh my god, I should totally know this. One forty? Or one fourteen? It's under Joshua Scott. He's my dad."

His fingers skate across the keyboard. "Sorry, I don't think that's it."

"Are you sure?"

More clicks of the keys, and a sigh. "No, it doesn't look like it." Now he's peering over the monitor at me, perhaps trying to remember if he's seen me check in.

Black panic coils up around me. What if, what if, what if . . .

"Or"—I suck in my breath—"could it be under my . . . other dad's name? Miles Faye? *He* could've, like, booked the room for us."

I wait for the clerk to wave me off, but he doesn't. "I've got a Miles Faye in room two fifty-six."

Oh thank god. I slap my forehead with my free hand. "I am *such* a flake. That's totally it."

"I'm guessing you'll want a spare key?"

"That would be *amazing*," I gush, collecting the key card from him after he feeds it through a little machine on the desk. "Thank you, thank you, thank you." I grin as brightly as possible and walk away, casually sipping my Coke.

Jessa would be proud, I think.

Back at the elevators I drain the soda—I could use the caffeine—and collect my things. I ride up to the narrow corridor of the second floor, where the wallpaper is the red-orange of a bright, bloody sunset. Just around the corner is room 256. A dull orange door like every door, except not. The key card is in my sweat-slick hand, but I'm afraid to use it.

I think it's like this: as long as you don't turn the last page in a book, you get to believe whatever you want to believe. You can have faith the good guys will win, the clearly identifiable bad guys will lose, and everyone will go home and eat Spicy Italians on flatbread on their cheerfully dumpy living room sofa. I'm not living in a sunshiny state of delusion. I know this is real life, not some story by Sir Arthur Conan Doyle or Agatha Christie or Rex Stout. Whatever's in room 256 will be in the room, whether I open the door or not.

But I am so fucking scared to turn the page.

When the key card slot blips green, I ease the handle down, peering into the dark behind the door. A wall of stale heat and the pretentious sweet-spicy smell of Djarum Blacks break over me.

Carefully, I make my way across the cluttered floor, to the single bed where a long lump under the sheets is illuminated in the slice of hallway light, and steady my voice.

"It's time to get up, Dad."

While my father splashes water on himself in the bathroom, I poke the toe of my boot through the debris of empty beer cans and fast-food delivery cartons covering the carpet. There are a lot more cans than cartons, but at least he's been eating. I'm reminded by my percolating stomach that I haven't, and none of the half-full boxes of rice or feebly rewrapped burgers look farm fresh. I sniff one—which has recently pulled double duty as an ashtray—then carefully pat the wrapper back in place.

He emerges in a dingy T-shirt and his old pinch-kneed sweatpants. He blinks in the lamplight, and I wonder where his glasses are. His black hair is wild and sopping. Droplets trickle through the dark scruff shadowing his cheeks and chin. As he stands there unshaven in sports-themed loungewear, reeking of clove cigarettes, it could almost be funny, except for how thin and grayish-pale and crumpled Dad looks, and how he eyes the covers like he'd love nothing more than to slip back under them and sleep.

To stop this from happening, I sit stiffly on the bed, fisting my hands in the papery brown sheets. I've been waiting for this moment, and now I don't know how to start.

Surprisingly, Dad does. "What are you doing here, Imogene." It's not even a question. More like a line in a script he has to read, instead of a topic of actual curiosity.

"What do you mean, what am I doing here? I followed you. The clues you left me."

He stares at me, almost-black eyes blank.

I dig through my bag, dumped at the foot of the bed,

and pull out the heart. "You left this for me, didn't you? To tell me where you'd gone? To tell me where I could find you?"

The longer the silence drags on, the more stupid my words sound echoing in my own ears.

"If you didn't want me to look for you, then why did you give me the heart?"

His hand rasps against thick stubble as he drags it down his face. "I don't know."

"You have to! You're the grown-up! Isn't it, like, your job to know what you're doing?"

Shrinking down onto the bed, he shuts his eyes. "Maybe—I just wanted you to have something from me."

"Why?" I ask, cold and quiet. "How long were you planning on being gone?"

He doesn't answer.

The blood is sort of fuzzing out of my brain and toes and fingers, so I can barely feel the roughness of the stone, or the sharpness of the crystals. Just a solid, unknowable weight. "I'm your *daughter*. Lindy is your *wife*. We were pretty much falling apart. And *this* is what you were gonna leave us with?" I hold it up for him to see.

Dad winces.

With all my strength I hurl the thing across the

room, against the wall. It dings the plaster and tiny chips of rock fly, but the geode rebounds and thumps to the floor, intact. "This is nothing!" I shriek. "It's a stupid fucking rock!"

"Imogene, stop!" he cries.

But I don't. I stomp on it with my winter boot, and it only grinds into the thin carpet. "It's a story! It isn't Mom and it isn't you and it doesn't mean shit! So I don't want it!" I don't even look so much as feel around the room for something heavy. I land on the squat brass lamp on the bedside table and heft it, knocking off the shade and lightbulb in one swipe.

"You'll hurt yourself," Dad protests.

With shaking hands I raise the lamp to bring the base down on the stone as hard as I can. There's a sound like splintering bone, and it caves. Furiously, I kick at the shards. Bits of crunched crystal and pulverized stone scatter across the carpet. I bring the lamp up again, but a sweaty band of strong fingers closes around my wrist.

"Stop, stop, stop," he hushes, like he's a father and I'm a newborn. Sitting back on the bed, Dad drops his head into his hands. "Uhssry," he mumbles.

"Huh?"

He lifts his chin. "I said I'm sorry."

"Good. So . . ." I set the lamp down and rub my palms on my pants legs. "Good." Joining him on the bed, I sit still for a minute before tipping my head against his shoulder, my nose squashed against his chest. He hesitates, then slings his arm around me, which puts this scratchy feeling in my throat.

"What are *you* doing here, Dad?"

Slowly he reaches into the pocket of sweatpants I'm positive he's been wearing for a longer stretch of time than is appropriate. He pulls out a piece of paper, one that's clearly been folded and unfolded and refolded times infinity until the creases have become needle-sharp, and hands it to me.

On it is a printed photo of my mother, of Sidonie Malachai, outside her peach-colored condo on Pines Road. It doesn't look like she knows her picture's being taken. Below it, a pageful of information is typed out—phone number, address, the name of the law firm she works for. Her husband's name.

"Last month I hired this PI," he says. "Guy I've consulted for my books a few times. Good at his job."

I don't know if I want to laugh or cry. "You're telling me you hired a detective? Like, paid some other guy to track Mom down?" I remember one of the few facts of Dad's disappearance. "What did it cost, fifteen hundred dollars?"

"Almost." He stares at my mother's picture while he speaks. "How did *you* find *me*?"

"Hard fucking work, and no cheating, that's how!"

"Don't swear, Imogene."

"What are you gonna do, send me to my hotel room?" But I don't want to hurt his feelings, so I press myself tighter against him and give him the short version.

Maybe I'm looking for a little admiration, a little *Boy, the apple doesn't fall far from the tree.* But I don't get it. "You shouldn't waste your life trying to save me," he says, and sighs. "I never wanted that. You don't deserve this."

"I mean, I'm on school vacation, so there's that. And I did other stuff. I slept over Jessa's. Played video games. Lost my prom date."

He jerks backward. "You have a prom date?"

"No." I smile tightly into his shoulder. "Keep up." We're quiet for a moment, the only sound in the room the out-of-beat percussion of the old heating system pumping out rusty-smelling air, and then I take a deep breath of cigarettes and unwashed Dad and ask, "Why did you need to see Mom so bad? You have me. And Lindy. We're not enough?"

"It wasn't like that," he says dully. "I was scared. Your mother . . . she always got to me. I'd be going along just fine, and then I'd look at the calendar and it'd be her birthday, or I'd pass a store and see her favorite color in the window. I'm not saying all the bad times were about her, but remembering her . . . it could get me down. And our anniversary was coming up, but I'd been so good for so long. With you, and with your stepmother. I thought if I could know about Sid, if she could stop being this question mark, if I could just *know*, then I would be all right. Officially, once and for all. I hired the PI, and then I knew what I knew, what I never quite expected, that she was married and happy, and I kept waiting for the crash. But it didn't come."

"That's a good thing, right? But . . . Dad, you seem a little . . . crashed."

He nods. "I wasn't, though. Not at first. Then I wondered, what if these aren't my real feelings? What if it's all just medication, and how would I know? Shouldn't I be feeling this? I thought that would be the real test."

"You stopped taking your meds," I guess. "Okay, I don't get it. Were you afraid you were going to crash, or afraid you weren't?"

Dad drops his head back into his hands. "Both. I know it doesn't make sense. I know you don't get it. I don't know how anyone could, if they haven't been through it."

"Like Mom has." The realization sinks through me like a stone. "That's why you wanted to find her. Not to save her or anything. Not like she needed it. Dad . . . you lied about the curse," I say gently. "My whole life, I've been doing things . . . the way I thought she wouldn't. Because I didn't want to be like Mom, and I thought if I tripped one time, I'd just keep falling, like she did."

"I shouldn't have put that on you." His breath hitches.

"But if you told me the truth about how bad it was for you, maybe I could've helped you."

"I don't know how. I don't know how I expected your mother to help me. I don't know how I *could* be helped."

It's the illness talking, I tell myself. It's not like I've never heard this before during the bad times. And Dad's right, I don't know what it's like to be sick that way.

But yeah, I get fear. I get being afraid that you don't have anything to say to people, so you never talk to people. I get never going to parties because you're afraid you won't fit in at the party. I get loving the same boy for eight years and never doing anything about it, but that's okay because part of the reason you love him is that he's always around for you to not do anything about. I get closing up your heart because you're afraid to look inside and find out it's hollow. I get choosing to be alone because you're afraid that if the choice is out of your hands, you'll simply be lonely, and alone is okay, it's almost cool, in a way. But loneliness isn't just being alone.

That's what my bedtime story taught me, anyway.
Except I'm not so sure. I think maybe fear is worse,
the useless kind that doesn't help you cram for a test or
jazz you up before bungee jumping, but sneaks in and
strangles you. My mom was so afraid her own daughter
would reject her, she never tried to find me, so she sat
alone with her sketchbook.

If she had been less afraid to be lonely . . . If Dad
hadn't let me believe it was the most awful thing
possible . . . If, if, if.

Whether it's dead or alive, we can't change the past.

There are a million more questions I could ask, the
whens and the hows and the whys. But whatever facts I
might collect, however I might chip away at the pain of
this past week, there's only a single "because" that really
matters. Because Dad isn't well right now, and there are
reasons for that, but no one perfect answer. So all of the
truths in the world aren't as important as this one:

"I want you to come home," I tell him. I thought
knocking on my mom's door was the hardest thing I'd
ever done, but as I sit up and look up at my dad and he
stares back at me, damp-eyed and wilting, I think this
might be it. "And I want you to take your meds and get
help again, for me. I know it's like . . . if you could fix
whatever was wrong by pouring dry cement . . . I'm not
saying it right. Just, I know it's really hard. But . . . I'm a

kid. You have to be around for me and take care of me. 'Cause you're my dad. And I love you and whatever."

"And whatever." He sniffles. "I'm not right, *bou bui*."

"I know. You'll come with me?"

"I'll come."

"Okay. Oh, except I don't exactly have a car, in the technical sense." Before he can change his mind or mine, I smudge the tears out of my eyes, pick up the telephone on the lampless nightstand, and dial our home number.

"Hel-lo?" a high-pitched, un-Lindy-ish voice answers cautiously.

"Jessa?"

"Imogene-*fucking*-Scott!" she screams into the speaker. "Where are you? You know everyone is going batshit over here?"

"Who's everyone?"

"Uh, your stepmother, for one? And your actual mom? And my mom? And *me*?"

She tells me the story of last night. How Lindy came home to an empty house around nine and knocked on the Prices' door right away, assuming I'd skipped out to see Jessa. Chad was staying overnight with Omar Wolcott in his dorm room at BU, and Jessa was on a date with Jeremy; still pissed after our fight, she'd officially gotten back together with him, to spite me (or so she says). They had gone to the movies in Framingham, and by the time they emerged from the theater and answered their phones, it was after ten. Under the pressure of Lindy's Authority Voice, Jessa folded like a paper airplane. She told my stepmother we'd been searching for Dad since the start of vacation, and in the process had found my real mother. After giving Lindy my mother's number, Jessa was promptly grounded for aiding and abetting.

It was midnight when Lindy called Sidonie, and by then I definitely should've made it back to Sugarbrook station. They compared notes and figured out pretty quickly that I was headed to Victory Island. This is when Lindy called the police.

"Ugh," I groan.

"As if she wouldn't," Jessa points out. "You're lucky there's not, like, an Amber Alert about you."

Who was called out of bed but Officer Griffin. She showed up in the early a.m. to interview Jessa and Lindy and assure them I couldn't have gotten as far as the island. Not a seventeen-year-old without a car, not in this weather. I was probably stuck at a station in between—probably in Boston—and they would notify the police right away to look out for me. Lindy was to stay by the phone. When Officer Griffin left to set things in motion, it was after five, and I was just about to board the early train from North Station to Newburyport.

Lindy did not stay by the phone. After a restless few hours, she asked Dr. Van Tassel to babysit the landline at 42 Cedar Lane, with Jessa keeping her mother company. Lindy was presently headed east to Victory Island to cruise along the beach.

"Huh." I struggle to take this all in while keeping an eye on Dad, now pacing back and forth in front of the curtained windows. "And where's your mom?"

"In the bathroom. I'm in your room. I was freaking out and just waiting, so I've been reading that book by your bed. *Rebecca*? Not super romantic."

"No, that's the cool thing! It's not about love, it's about obsession. Rebecca-the-person was horrible, but Rebecca-the-mystery was this fixation that almost kept this girl from loving and being loved. It's like a mystery about the dangers of a mystery and—" I notice Dad watching me. "Never mind. Not the time for this. Can you tell your mom we're okay? I should probably call Lindy ASAP."

"Wait, we? You found your dad? You actually found him?"

I smile, though she can't see. "I did. Look, Jessa, I'm sorry I was so horrible and you were all going batshit. You're a really great friend."

"Me too. I am also sorry that you were so horrible."

"Hmm. See you when I'm not grounded?"

"Yeah," she says, and laughs. "We should be in our late thirties by then. I love you, Im."

After that, the only thing left to do is call Lindy's cell and ask for her help, so I do, and she yells a little and cries a little and so do I, and then I ask her to come get us and take us home.

NINETEEN

Because you can't lie to your stepmother over and over again, break into a hospital records storage room, drive all across the state with ill-gotten funds, skip town on a Greyhound without telling anyone, spend the night in a Boston train station, strike out for the coast all on your own, *and* face zero consequences, I am indeed grounded for quite a while. School is allowed, as are trips to a family therapist with Dad and Lindy, and, shockingly, visits with Jessa once her own punishment is lifted. But aside from seeing the ex–Sugarbrook Sandpipers as they filter in and out of the Prices' home, my first brush with the public comes over three months later. Prom night.

The theme turns out to be "A Night Among the Stars." Except the prom committee must've reached a stalemate when trying to decide which stars we'd be spending the night among. Exhibit A: when we pull up to Crystal Peak, a big glass banquet hall that's the second-nicest in Sugarbrook, cardboard cutouts of paparazzi are propped outside the entrance, crowded around the faux-crystal columns, hunched behind cardboard cameras. Meanwhile, gold and silver stars dangle from the ceiling of the portico overhead.

"This"—Chad twists around in the driver's seat of his mom's Solstice—"is the classiest goddamn soiree I've ever seen. You think they'll serve Grey Poupon?"

"I bet that joke would be funny if we were old and uncool." Jessa stands in the backseat beside me, sliding gracefully over the side without using the door, floor-length dress and all. A block back, she asked Chad to pull over and put the convertible top down for our big entrance, than coast fifteen miles per hour the rest of the way so we'd arrive unruffled. I follow through the actual door and join her, my low heels clomping on the pavement.

Chad flips his sunglasses up onto his head to look at us. "You girls are heartbreakers," he says, sweetly and sincerely.

I blush; old habit. Jessa is beautiful, right at home among the paper paparazzi. Her plum-purple dress has a deep neckline, with a drop waist that hugs her body all the way down till just above her knees, where it flares gently out and pools around her pale gold pumps. I don't know how she can dance in it, but as Jessa demonstrated to the seizing beats of Nicki Minaj in her bedroom, dance she can. A knotted gold chain glitters below her collarbone. Her red-gold hair, parted deep to the side, floats in finger waves over her shoulders.

I'm wearing my Suzanne's Dress for Less purchase, wine red, with its full knee-length skirt swinging. Fabulous Aunt Annette, enlisted as our stylist for the evening, gave me a coiled updo pinned into a side bun, a dark red lip, and a light smoky eye. And because we didn't know the etiquette for corsages versus boutonnieres when your prom date is in fact your best friend, we're both wearing matching corsages with white roses.

"Can you pick us up at midnight? At Mackenzie Winn's?" Jessa asks her brother. Mackenzie's throwing a post-prom bonfire, to which the elite of mock trial—and probably half the class—have been invited.

"Anything for you two." Chad winks and flips his glasses down. They're mostly unnecessary now that the sun is setting, but he's still handsome and blond and almost as perfect as ever.

"Nerd!" Jessa shouts affectionately as he drives off through an obstacle course of sparkling and tuxedoed seniors. Chad's our extra-generous chauffer tonight. Maybe because he's grateful we never implicated him in our schemes. Maybe because he felt guilty/thankful/confused (or disappointed?) when I relieved him of his prom duties. Maybe because we are heartbreakers. I could spend hours unpacking Chadwick Price's motives, but that's another habit I'm trying to kick. It's getting easier. Like, Omar Wolcott asked me to come out with him to the Friendly Toast once I was ungrounded and released back into the wild, and when I breezily informed Chad, I did not pause to dissect the arc of his eyebrow or analyze the downward curve of his full mouth, millimeter by millimeter. And when he and Pari split awkwardly apart after two months of winky faces, I didn't even gloat.

Progress! Personal growth!

Beyond the big glass double doors of Crystal Peak, inside the big glass foyer, an actual photographer in a white tux starts to take our picture. "Wait!" Jessa says. Looking deeply bored, he lowers his camera while Jessa turns to me, patting her hair smooth with one palm. "How do I look?"

I give her the compliment I think will mean the most to her. "You look just like Taylor Swift."

"Seriously?" She beams.

"What about me?"

"Perfect. You're so elegant! Like a sexy Asian Kate Middleton!"

We wrap our arms around each other's bare shoulders, shivering a little in the overcool air-conditioning inside the hall, and smile through our goose bumps.

"One more!" she cries, folding one slim, perfectly spray-tanned arm around the back of my neck and the other around my waist to dip me. I lift my lacy black kitten heel off the floor like I'm so flustered by the butterflies of love, I can't keep both feet on the ground.

The flash pops. "Okay, okay," the photographer dismisses us.

We head into the main hall, where Exhibit B: a plush red carpet stretches from the entrance across the parquet dance floor to the buffet table in back of the long room. Over the table a *Welcome, Sugarbrook High* banner hangs from the ceiling, midnight blue, painted with planets.

Puzzling theme decorations aside, Crystal Peak is actually beautiful. Set away from the road on a wooded hill off Acorn Drive, it's surrounded on all sides by towering pin oaks, and the sun slanting through the trees casts green leaf light through the floor-to-ceiling windows. Out back is a patio where kids are taking pictures. "Want to go see?" I ask. We make our way across the dance floor, still sparsely populated because it's early. Jessa pauses to say hello to loads of people—mostly drooling boys—and I wave to a few of them. I even accept a hug from Katie Rodriguez in her sparkly, sky-blue ball gown.

"You're like an Urban Outfitters model, Imogene!" she assures me.

"You too, definitely. But prettier."

"Oh my god, that's so sweet!"

I don't really know her. I don't know many of them, even after twelve years in the same small schools, twelve years of going to the same pizza parties and joining the same extracurriculars. But I kind of love them in the fuzzy, glowing, Barbara Walters camera filter of graduation and permanent good-byes. I wish I'd known it would be like this. I wish I'd gotten to know them, let them get to know me.

I'll do better at college, I promise myself. I'll have to—at the end of August, while I'm moving into my dorm room at Emerson College in Boston, Jessa will set out for the Savannah College of Art and Design in Georgia. She hasn't picked a discipline yet, but she'll figure it out. She's her own kind of genius, my best friend.

Stopping at the buffet to grab plastic flutes of "champagne" that tastes spot-on for ginger ale, we slide open the glass patio doors and go into the flushed early June air. Flattening our dresses under our butts, we perch on a bench facing west, where the evening sun bobs pink and orange over the silhouetted treetops.

A few yards away, Lee Jung and his sophomore girl-friend, Cassidy Meyer, lean against the railing, holding their phones with outstretched arms and snapping pictures of themselves kissing with the sunset behind them. Her hair is braided in a stiff, bejeweled halo; his is gelled into a black slick. Between tonguing and posing, Lee catches sight of me. He flushes, looks away, and hurries Cassidy back inside.

"Like, there but for the grace of god goes you," Jessa snickers.

"He was nice. Sweaty hands, though. No taste in music. He put Chris Brown on my mix CDs."

Shaking our heads, we gulp our champale.

My cell phone vibrates inside the impractically small and beautifully beaded clutch Lindy gave me. One of the conditions of my freedom is I have to check in frequently. I don't really mind. I mean, I know I'm supposed to think it's annoying and overprotective, but Lindy says family isn't blood, necessarily; it's a thousand little choices we make every day. We choose to trust each other and forgive each other and go to the pasta place for dinner even though some of us would rather eat sushi. Dad didn't choose to be sick, but he chose to go back to therapy and take his meds and to be there for us. And maybe I didn't choose to have an around-the-corner-from-average family, or to get a new stepmother when I was in high school, but I can choose to stick by her while Dad's getting better. I'm trying to let her in, like I know she wants me to. When I opened the door of the Tiki Motel room to see Lindy standing there, I thought she'd run straight to Dad. She loves him, after all. But the first thing she did was pull me in and crush me against her for a long moment, muttering into my ear, "If you *ever* scare me like that again, Imogene Mei Scott, I will have you surgically attached to me."

I'm glad she and Dad have each other.

The text is a picture message from Dad, clearly taken by Lindy. He sits in his big red armchair, toasting with a wineglass full of fruit punch (the carton is clearly visible beside him). Below is the caption: *Enjoy your big night, Immy. Be smart. Tell the boys you're saving all your dances for Jesus.*

I text back: *Safe at the prom. Enjoy your Hitchcock marathon, party animals. Love you.*

Jessa leans in to read over my shoulder. "Aww!"

"Yeah, we're precious. What's Jeremy doing tonight?"

"Probably staring at my picture for hours without

blinking." She smiles and bats her eyelashes.

I *want* to say he couldn't possibly, unless it was taped to his mirror. Except making fun of Jeremy is such a low-hanging fruit, it's practically a potato. What matters is that he makes her happy (even when he makes her miserable, I guess).

As the sun flares in our eyes, Jessa swats away a small cloud of gnats—it's a fact of life that Sugarbrook is beset by them every time the weather warms—then hooks her arm around mine. "I'm gonna miss you, Im."

"Me too. A lot."

"But I'll be back for every single vacation."

"And until then, every painting you make can be of my exquisite face."

"Yeah, and, like, your first literary masterpiece can be all about me!"

"Oh, definitely."

She pries her iPhone from her own tiny purse and aims it at me. "Want to take a picture to send to your mom?"

I shrug. I don't know if we're at a selfie-sharing phase in our relationship. I've seen her once since February: the week after Dad came home, when she drove up to Sugarbrook to see him. I don't know what they talked about—they went into the office and shut the doors behind them—but it wasn't a long visit, and he seemed okay when she left. He came out and patted my cheek, then took his pre-dinner pills. While he brewed his customary six o'clock coffee, I finally got around to asking why he'd lied about he and Mom being married.

He watched the coffee trickle down into the pot. "I guess I wanted you to think you'd had a perfectly normal family once, even if you couldn't remember it. Pretty dumb, huh, *bou bui*?"

I swallowed and leaned into him. "Yeah, Dad."

Then Lindy came in, and I helped her chop asparagus tips into precise segments, as instructed, and the three of us sat down to eat, like every night.

Lindy says it's my choice to forgive Mom, and I guess I have. At least I'm trying to, though I don't know if we'll ever be perfectly comfortable with each other.

But even at the end of a mystery, everything's not perfect, you know? The dead stay dead, no matter that the murderer's been caught. The main character finds her answer, but maybe it's not the right one; maybe the question she had in her head from the start was all wrong, and now she has to live with the weight of what she knows and what she'll never know. I mean, look at *Rebecca*. Even though Manderley burns down, and long after the place of all her and Maximilian de Winter's suffering has crumbled into a cold pile of ash and blackened stones on a lonely beach, it still haunts the unnamed heroine. She still dreams of it in the end of her story.

Obviously, I'm just graduating high school, so it's not exactly the end of my story.

I freeze a smile in place, and Jessa takes the picture.

The music picks up inside, pounding out through the walls behind us. We twist around to watch our classmates drift toward the dance floor, summoned by the pied piper of a Kesha song on full volume. Levi Cantu waves at Jessa from the buffet table, sets his champale down, and pantomimes his intentions with sharp, sprinkler-armed moves.

She turns to me, her thin shoulders swaying slightly to the beat. "We can stay out here a little longer. However long you want."

"No, let's go in. The bugs are out anyway."

"Yeah?"

We stand and smooth our dresses down and catch sight of our faint reflections in the glass, side by side.

"Are you ready?" she asks.

I open the door.

REBECCA PODOS is a graduate of
the writing, literature, and publishing program
at Emerson College, where she won the MFA award
for best thesis. Her fiction has been published in
Glimmer Train, *Glyph*, *Paper Darts*, *Bellows
American Review*, and *SmokeLong Quarterly*.
She lives with her husband in Connecticut.
The Mystery of Hollow Places is her first novel.